# WICKED DECEIT

## SAM WICK UNIVERSE THRILLER #1

### CHASE AUSTIN

THRILLVERSE PUBLISHING

# ABOUT WICKED DECEIT

**What do you do when your own President wants you dead? You call Sam Wick.**

*SPECIAL OFFER - GET THE NEXT 2 SAM WICK UNIVERSE THRILLERS WITH THIS BOOK. DETAILS INSIDE.*

*Sam Wick is the one the Government calls on to extract people out of the worst of the worst enemy places on earth. Where the government cannot and will not go, he will. There is no guarantee that he'll succeed every time but he doesn't have a choice or does he?*

✓ His mission: Extract Carlos Cruz-Diez—a New York Times reporter from the clutches of death.

✓ Location: Venezuela Consulate in Vienna, Austria.

✓ The obstacle: Venezuela's National Intelligence Service has sent sixteen of their best to execute this mission.

✓ Timeline: Twenty-four hours.

Time is running out. Bullets are flying. Bodies are piling up. Nothing is as it seems. Will Sam Wick succeed?

If you like Tom Clancy's Jack Ryan, Ted Bell's Alex Hawke, Lee Child's Jack Reacher, Vince Flynn's Mitch Rapp, WEB Griffin's Killer McCoy, Stephen Hunter's Bob Lee Swagger, and Robert Ludlum's Jason Bourne, you will love Sam Wick.

# YOUR FREEBIE

*Do not forget to download your FREE COPY of The NSA Top Secret Report on SAM WICK.*

*Details at the end of this book.*

# CHAPTER 1

What could you possibly offer the man who controlled not only your destiny but that of your whole country? The man who ruled with an iron fist. The man who had the Russian President on his speed-dial. The man who had once given the finger to the US President at a diplomatic convention. What could you possibly give the President of your country on his birthday?

But Henrique Arias Cárdenas, the director of the Venezuela Intelligence Service, had more on his mind than a birthday present while he waited in the visitor's lounge of the Palacio de Miraflores—the President of Venezuela's office. He glanced at the 19th-century wall clock above the majestic office door behind which the President was about to meet him. It was thirteen past two in the morning and the city was quiet after a long day of travails, but Henrique wasn't even thinking of sleep. There wasn't any time. He sat at the edge of the couch with his back straight, his hands sweating even in the temperature-controlled room.

Since his phone rang an hour ago, he was racking his brain to construe a reason for the urgency of this meeting but got nothing. Not a pleasant situation to be in, especially for the Director of Venezuela's premier intelligence agency.

He already had a meeting scheduled with the President at eight in the morning, just before the whole country would start celebrating their leader's birthday. Festivities had been planned for the next seven days, and over the past few weeks, he and his men had been busy foiling the attempts by radical extremists to devise disruptions in the celebrations. His office had been diligent in sending daily briefs to the President's office. What then had warranted this late-night summons? What was it that could not wait for six more hours?

One of the officers standing alert near the grand door lifted his right hand to his earpiece and then glanced at Henrique. It was time.

As Henrique fell in step with his escort, he coughed twice, attempting to relax the lump in his throat. It didn't work. He took his hands out of his trouser pockets to reduce the sweating; that didn't work either. Then the big gates opened before him and it was too late to do anything. He took a deep breath and hoped for the best.

.   .   .

The President was standing at the royal desk, his fingers resting on a folded publication. Henrique walked in and stopped at a respectful distance, carefully observing the President's face to gauge his mood. The man was not just upset; he was seething with anger.

He glanced at the publication in the President's hand and recognized the font. It was a copy of the New York Times. He said nothing. The President's laser-focused stare was unsettling, making him unsure of his next steps.

"Venezuela is a mess, a bloody mess." His boss read out the front-page headline, looking straight at him. He jerked his hand, and the newspaper slid across the table to Henrique who stopped it, with a swift gesture, quickly glancing at the columnist's name—Carlos Cruz-Díez. "You know why he can so boldly accuse us of these baseless charges?"

Henrique appeared alarmed by the anger but maintained a stoic silence. It was a rhetorical question.

"I should have killed him. I should have killed him and hanged him for others to see and learn, instead of letting him leave the country."

"We can still do it." Henrique finally had something to offer.

.   .   .

"How?"

"He visited our consulate in Vienna a few days ago."

"Why did no one tell me that?"

"It was in the PDB," Henrique said, referring to the President's daily brief sent by his office.

The President considered it for a moment.

"How soon?"

"He is going to visit again. We can take care of him then if you want."

"How?"

"It's better if you remain unaware of the modalities."

The President weighed this momentarily-Plausible deniability-before a slow smile appeared on his lips. Henrique smiled too. This was his birthday present to the President.

# CHAPTER 2

Team Vesuvius was already in the briefing room when Sam Wick arrived. The three Vesuvius members - Jessica, Stan, and Mac - looked up as he entered. Their tense postures relaxed slightly at the sight of a familiar face. Wick scanned the space. It was a boardroom kind of setting with a long wide conference table at its center, surrounded by twelve mid-back mesh desk chairs. The wall opposite to the door doubled up as a projector screen. He instinctively walked towards the chair that had clear visibility of both the projector screen and the exit. Sitting down, he observed the others in the room.

Team Vesuvius was one of Task Force 77's (TF-77) support teams. TF-77 was a black ops team jointly created by the NSA and the US Army - an off-the-books team that comes into play when the diplomatic solutions failed. Powered with US military might across the globe and NSA's intel, the team was well equipped to handle anything and that made it the one to go for the toughest missions on the most dangerous locations using means that any government would never authorize yet expect it to get done. During these deadly missions the TF-77's assets, like Sam Wick, were supported by small on-the-ground teams like Vesuvius. These teams typically comprise three to four members—made available to field operatives depending on their mission.

Jessica led the Vesuvius. She was the logistics liaison and an expert in close combat. Stan was a former marine and an Olympic-level shooter. Mac was the go-to guy for anything remotely associated with technology. Together these three represented one of TF-77's ace support teams.

Wick knew of the Vesuvius team and each one of its members. Though nothing in his expression showed it, he was glad he would be going into this mission with them.

# CHAPTER 3

VESUVIUS KNEW OF WICK TOO. His reputation in the field preceded him. At 5'11", he had a weather-beaten face that had a rugged attraction, not least because of his unreadable sea-blue eyes, bright with intelligence. With his slicked-back black hair and athletic build, he seemed like a man on a mission. He'd been born in Kansas, but he spoke with a neutral accent, due to his extended stay in Afghanistan, Iraq, and Pakistan.

He was the man to whom TF-77 assigned its most insane and impossible missions and, so far, he had emerged from each in one piece. He talked less, absorbed more, and did his job with brutal competence. He had gone from ninety successful extractions to over three hundred in just over half a decade. Just twenty-seven years old, he was not flamboyant in the way many other operatives his age were. He [vb1] preferred simple, time-tested tactics over ones that dropped jaws, but he kept pulling off incredible feats - no matter the opposition, no matter the conditions, no matter the situation. His strategies and tactics were already turning into TF-77 mission case studies on whether brilliance could be achieved without being adventurous. Team Vesuvius—Jessica, in [AU2] particular—had seen all this in a few of her past missions with Sam. She was content that for this mission he was the chosen one.

▭

The door opened, and Andrew McAvoy entered. He was the keeper of this safe house and part of the mission control team of TF-77.

"Good morning everyone." McAvoy greeted them, walking straight to the laptop sitting at the end of the table. There were muted responses all around.

McAvoy keyed in his password and the wall lit up with an image of a middle-aged man looking at them through a pair of gold-rimmed reading glasses.

"Carlos Cruz-Díez," he said, pointing to the image on the screen. "Born and bred in Venezuela, Carlos is a prominent human rights activist and a columnist for major publications. For decades he was close to the Venezuela leadership, serving as a government adviser, but fell out of favor and went into self-imposed exile in the U.S.A. last year. From there, he has been writing monthly columns in the New York Times and occasionally for the Washington Post, criticizing the policies of the Venezuela President. Tomorrow morning, he is scheduled to visit the Venezuela

Consulate in Vienna to get certain documents certifying that he has renounced his Venezuelan citizenship. His appointment is with Ana Sofía, Minister-Counsellor at the consulate, who helped him during his last visit too." He paused. "According to our source, this time Venezuela is planning to do something major in the consulate involving Carlos. He has been extremely vocal against the regime of his country, and that's why he is important to us in our support for the human rights groups in Venezuela. All this means his country's President isn't happy with him. Also, we have been trying to bring the Venezuela President to the negotiation table for months now. Till now he's been a tough nut to crack. POTUS is not very happy with the way they are summarily turning down our requests for talks. We believe intercepting this planned act can give us an opening to bring them in the same room. Your job is to find everything about this plan and if there is a danger to Carlos' life, then get him out of there, preferably alive. Any questions?"

Hands shot up. McAvoy pointed at Stan to go ahead.

"When was his last visit?"

"He visited the consulate seven days ago along with his fiancée, Karina Anez, when he was asked to come back again in a week to collect the signed documents."

"Did anything suspicious happen during the last visit?" Stan asked the follow-up question.

.   .   .

"According to our source, he walked into the consulate quite confidently because he believes nothing untoward can happen to him on Austrian soil. He reportedly told his friends he had been treated "very warmly" on his first visit and reassured them he did not face any problems. During his last visit, however, he gave Ms. Anez, his fiancée, two cell phones and told her to call someone close to the Austrian President if he did not come out within a reasonable timeframe. So it seems he does harbor some doubts."

"How long has he been in a relationship with this woman?" Mac asked next.

"Just over a year."

"Who are the usual suspects here?"

"The Venezuela intelligence agency, specifically its director, Henrique Arias Cárdenas. His team had been surveilling Carlos and Karina for the last three months."

"So why are we acting now?"

"This time their President seems to have lost his patience. He is pretty riled up by the negative publicity he is attracting because of Carlos' articles on his government's repression of dissent, often through violent crackdowns on street protests, the jailing of opponents, and the prosecution of civilians in the military courts. His columns have consistently raised concerns about poor prison conditions, impunity for human rights violations, and harassment by government officials of human rights activists and independent media outlets. Even Russia, Venezuela's closest ally, has asked them to take remedial measures. This seems to have blown their President's fuse. He met Henrique two days ago and has been assured by Henrique that Carlos will be taken care of. How and why? We don't know for sure yet."

McAvoy tapped the keypad. A new image appeared on the screen of a rugged face with a deep scar running from the right side of the temple to the jaw. There was no name on the photo. "This is one of the best-known operatives of the Venezuela Intelligence Service and we suspect that he will be leading this." McAvoy clicked again, and a new grainy image showed the same man walking past a large signboard of the Vienna International Airport. He wore a large brown hoodie and military boots, his hands in his pocket. A small carry bag was slung over his shoulder. "This photo was taken at eight this morning outside the departure gate." He clicked again. The next image showed the same man getting into a Toyota. "We have run the license plate." He clicked again. "This is the photo of the car's driver who picked him up from the airport." McAvoy paused and let the team absorb the details of the second man on the screen: clean shaven, trimmed hairs, no visible scar marks. There was a mole just under his right eye. "His name is Felipe Massa, a known operative of the Venezuela Intelligence Service in Austria who works under the cover of a travel agency."

.  .  .

"How reliable is this Venezuela source of yours?" Jessica asked.

"He is someone deeply rooted in Venezuela political circles and has been a critical asset for us in the past too."

"How do you want this to go down?" Wick asked.

"Venezuela has been a blow-hot, blow-cold ally for quite some time now, so this has to be dealt discreetly. No big bang please." McAvoy clicked and the image on the screen changed. "This is the front of Venezuela Consulate in Vienna. The building is at the Prinz Eugen-Straße. The number of personnel of Venezuelan descent are somewhere around fifteen, including the Ambassador. The rest of the staff consists of locals. Names, addresses, and photos of everyone on the staff are in the manila folders in front of you. You'll also find the blueprint of the building in there. In Vienna, Jakob is our asset who will be your driver and the single point of contact for ammunition, cash, id proofs and anything you need. He will also get your things transported into the consulate. In case anything goes wrong, he is the man you can rely on to get you out." McAvoy paused to see if anyone had any questions. "A private jet will take off from the Spangdahlem Air Base at 1200 hours. That gives you fifty-three minutes from now," he continued. "Any questions?"

There were none.

.  .  .

"People, ideally we would like you to get in and out as quickly as possible. We'd like to be able to play this off as a minor skirmish rather than a full-blown operation," he added, looking at Wick. "All the best."

# CHAPTER 4

VENEZUELA CONSULATE, **Vienna, Austria**

The corner office Ana Sofía was walking towards, was her next step on the corporate ladder. For the last nine months, ever since she had been posted here, she had set her sights on the chair that lay behind the heavy doors, the chair on which her boss currently sat.

A tall brunette, Ana walked right past the two administrative assistants and the security officers and entered the ambassador's office without asking for permission. Once inside, she closed the heavy door and approached her boss's desk, which was the size of an aircraft carrier.

She had a certain air of confidence about her, a sense of purpose to her every step. Her instincts about her surroundings were bang-on. As a minister-counselor in Venezuela's consulate in Austria, she had perfected the art of walking the thin rope between expectations and reality.

She was a fighter. Her struggles had started the day she graduated from the Universidad Central de Venezuela (Central University of Venezuela) thirteen years ago, and she'd been fighting ever since. Her rise to the top was a testament to her spirit, but it also signified the tough road to the top faced by women all over her country.

Her hatred of losing pushed her more than her desire to win. This was key to understanding what made her tick.

Men found her irresistible. Some found her harsh and even more were taken aback by her brash tactics, but she only cared about those who mattered to her in the larger scheme of things. Graceful at 5"10', with the legs of a Nordic goddess, and eyes like Audrey Hepburn's, she tended to dress conservatively—sober pantsuits, skirts stopping slightly above knee, black hair pulled back in a low ponytail—yet she wasn't afraid to sex up her look when she knew it would be worth the effort.

Her road to glory had been paved with some not very laudable moments—including some one-night stands with her ex-bosses, the last one being more than seven years ago.

Some of them had been insipid, while a few were extremely torrid—some of the best sex she'd ever had, and definitely the best sex they'd ever had. She wasn't ashamed of them but preferred not to repeat them as she gained more and more confidence and subtlety in her dealings with power.

But each encounter came with a deal. A deal to ensure that her star would not stop rising. And rise she did. Still, in her mid-thirties, Ana was now very close to her ambition of becoming an ambassador. She now stood before the man whose job she planned on taking soon.

Carpio was on the phone, and from his end of the conversation, she knew he was talking to a person of importance, but not the President. His voice was measured, and he was listening, instead of indulging his usual habit of dominating the conversation.

Carpio frowned as Ana entered his office without knocking, but she remained unfazed and there was little he could do about it. She took blatant advantage of his weakness in indulging her. To give credit where it was due, she did have an uncanny knack for getting things done, and for that she was invaluable. There was also excitement and apprehension associated with her. She was like a commanding hurricane, and he relished the power to control that hurricane if and when he wanted to. That was the reason he put up with her tantrums.

Carpio replaced the handset, wondering if he should tell Ana about the next day. She would get to know of it for sure, but he wanted to tell her himself, just to see how she would respond to the unexpected tidings.

He had barely put the receiver down when she started right off the bat, "Have you seen the ratings? They are a fucking disaster! The President is going to lose." She waved her hand in the air for emphasis. "And when that happens, you, me, and everyone else are going to be thrown to the wolves. What do you plan to do when the shit hits the fan?" Ana felt the odd feeling of someone else watching her. She turned and found two men sitting on the presidential couch in the corner, away from the desk and the door. There was no way she could have seen them sitting there, yet there they were. Instinctively her demeanor changed. She stared at the one who had a scar running from the right side of his temple to his jaw and felt a sense of unease.

"Ana, meet Joaquin and Felipe. They are here at the President's request." Carpio gestured at the two men while he peered at her face and decided to curb his instincts to tell her anything. She would be fine without this little piece of information.

# CHAPTER 5

INSIDE THE AIRCRAFT, Wick sat in the front, far away from his nearest neighbor Mac, who was keenly watching his every move.

"Stop staring at him like that," Stan whispered, nudging Mac.

"He is weird."

"None of our business."

"What if he gets us all killed?"

"You are not going in there with him, Jessica and I are."

. . .

"What if he gets you killed?" Mac asked.

"Not gonna happen," Stan whispered.

"How can you be so sure?"

"Shut up and do what Jessica asked you to."

"You mean what he asked for, through Jessica." Mac murmured.

"Whatever, just do it."

"Yeah, whatever." Mac refocused on the laptop screen

"How far are you from hacking into the consulate server?" Jessica asked. She was sitting right behind the two of them and had overheard their conversation.

"Not very. Will be done once we land."

Wick opened his eyes, turned around and gazed straight at Mac. "Can you extract the details of all the passengers from Venezuela who have landed in Vienna over the last forty-eight hours?"

.   .   .

"Yeah, sure." Mac felt naked to the stare. Wick had that effect on people as if he knew their darkest secrets.

"Thanks," Wick said and turned around. He didn't smile, didn't say anything else.

Mac shook his head and peered back at the laptop screen. Jessica glanced at Wick who was checking his phone. She had worked with him a couple of times in the past. But this time he seemed a bit off. She didn't know what to make of her observations but decided to keep her thoughts to herself.

In thirty minutes, they were going to land at Vienna International Airport.

## CHAPTER 6

THE STILLNESS in the air was in stark contrast to the storm brewing inside Wick. The information he had come across during his just-concluded mission in Poland had shaken him to the core. He wasn't one to be easily perturbed, but what he had learned had made him question his very existence.

Flashes from his childhood swirled in his mind. He had been an orphan as far back as he could remember. He had struggled through boarding school, bullied and beaten mercilessly at times. What made it worse was he had no one to write home to, to ask for advice or simply to vent his frustrations. He also had no friends, no bond with anyone at school. An average student, his presence or the lack of it made no impact on anyone, anywhere. He used to try to imagine how his parents might have looked by conjuring images out of thin air based on some distant memory, but nothing ever materialized from his efforts.

.   .   .

From as far back as he could remember, his only real connection to the outside world was a PO box. On the fifth of every month there was an envelope with his name on it, with enough bills tucked inside to sustain him over the next thirty days. There were never any sender's details on it. If he needed more money, he had to put a requesting letter in the same box with the reason and the date by which he needed it and the money reached him within the next seven days. He had done that only once in his life, just to see if someone would actually respond to his letter. He got the money by the sixth day. Never did it again.

He had originally tried to find the man who sent him the money, kept an eye on the post office during his days off, but never spotted anyone suspicious. After some time he made peace with the situation. It wasn't worth it. Whoever his patron was, he clearly wasn't interested in meeting him in person.

Around his fifteenth birthday, along with the cash, he received a note and a West Point Military Academy brochure. The crux of the letter was that his benefactor wanted him to go to the West Point next. If he decided not to pursue that career option, he was free to seek his interests elsewhere, but without the monthly financial aid. Sam checked the brochure. Relevant pages and sentences had already been marked. He had to respond within the next twenty-four hours, writing his answer on the back of the same letter, and placing it back in the box in the same envelope.

Sam had not thought about his career options till then and, despite the fact that the choice had literally been shoved down his throat by dangling a financial carrot, he found that he kind of liked the prospect of being in the forces. One of the reasons was that they would teach him to fight. If nothing else, it would be satisfying to get even with his bullies in the language they knew. It didn't take him twenty-four hours to respond. The next communication was on the usual date, and it gave him a list of resources and instructions about the things he needed to do to get into the academy. From that day, getting into the academy became his only goal.

His life became a whirlwind after that. Eventually, to protect his sanity, he had to stop thinking about his parents and about that mystery patron. The monthly communication stopped the day he graduated from the academy and was commissioned as a second lieutenant in the US army.

His life had been very busy since then, getting dropped into dangerous places and then trying to get out of there alive. Until two weeks ago. He had been sent to Poland. His job was to extract a man called Albert who was being held captive by the Polish Mafia. The mission wasn't a complete success. When Wick had found him, he had already been injected with a lethal virus. Despite the best efforts of a team of doctors, couldn't make it to US soil, succumbing during the journey.

The scene was still vivid in his memory.

Lying on a bed, Albert was studying Wick, who was resting on a nearby chair, examining the doctor's report. The attending nurse had gone for a coffee break. The doctor had left just before her.

There was nothing they could do. Albert was at a point of no return. Wick was frustrated, but he had done what he was ordered to do and could do nothing more.

For Wick, there was no despair in death. It had lost its shock value a long time ago. He had seen too much bloodshed on the battlefield for a dying man whom he had only known for the last eight hours to have much impact on his psyche. He had no idea why Albert had needed to be extracted. He cared little about the motives of his bosses as long as he got enough intel to survive in the battlefield. That was why he was such an important asset for the TF-77. He was clinical and asked few questions, a requirement for this kind of job.

Albert recognized his end was near. The virus had already consumed his liver and lungs to the point of no salvage. He had expected to meet his creator in that dank cell, but Wick and the doctors had extended his life, even though only by a few hours. But he couldn't just die, not just yet. Not after seeing Wick.

He made a growling sound and waved a weak hand, gesturing for Wick to come closer. Wick was surprised, but he got up and approached the stretcher.

Death made one rest one's hopes on the slimmest possibility. Albert was at that stage and Wick could understand. He knelt beside the stretcher and leaned forward to hear what the man had to say.

. . .

"Remember… me?" the man asked

Wick had no idea what he was talking about. He hadn't even known of the man's existence till about eight hours ago. The confusion must have been evident on his face because Albert's expression changed.

"Your… father… knows… me." Each word was a struggle.

"My father."

"Worked… with… him… long… ago."

Wick still had no idea what the man was talking about. "Do you know me? Who's my father?"

This time it was Albert who was surprised. He didn't know what to say next. Was he wrong about this man's identity? Maybe he wasn't the one. Maybe he had made a mistake.

"Did… you… go to West… Point?" he uttered each syllable very slowly.

"Yes."

.   .   .

"0...9...1...3...2...7... you... know... that?" The man had begun to shiver, his breathing shallow.

"How do you know that?" It was the code to Wick's locker at West Point. No one knew about it, even at the academy.

"Your... father."

"My father," Wick asked. "Who is he?"

"He... came... with... the... President?" The man was now rambling as if in his sleep, his eyes wandering aimlessly.

"President?"

"Your mother... good. Your father... killer." The man was speaking almost to himself now.

"Doctor!" Wick shouted looking at the door, then turned back to the man. "Albert, talk to me! Who are my parents?" Albert was losing consciousness. Wick got up and rushed to the door to see if the doctor was on his way.

"Lau...ren," the man murmured. His eyes closed, his fists clenched as if he was trying to avert death.

.   .   .

"Lauren!" Wick hurried back to him. "Who's Lauren? Is she my mother? What's her last name?" Wick grabbed Albert by his shoulders and jerked his weak body, trying to resuscitate him. "Doctor!" he screamed again. A man appeared at the door. The nurse followed him.

"He is dying," Wick yelled at him. "I need him to breathe for five minutes, that's all I need. Do something." Wick turned back to the dying man. "Albert, who's my father? Who's Lauren? What's her last name? Speak, look at me..." but Albert wasn't responding. He couldn't anymore. His eyes had started to bleed, his tongue was curled upwards, his gaunt face was expressionless.

Wick stared at his dead body. The doctor checked his pulse. "I'm sorry," he said.

Wick showed no emotion. The man who was yelling a moment ago silently gazed at Albert who hadn't meant anything to him a few minutes ago. The doctor and the nurse looked at him with apprehension. The silence was unsettling, as if something in Wick had simply switched off. Wick said nothing for the rest of the flight. And when the plane landed, he was the first one to get out. He didn't wait for the body to be picked up. He reported to the base and then left for the safehouse.

So his childhood was nothing but a lie. He had to do *something*! But what? Was his mother still alive? Lauren. Was she even his mother, married to his father? If Albert knew him and his parents, then there must be others too. This revelation had turned his world upside down. The sense of betrayal was unbearable. They had given birth to him and then left him to die. Why? Was he born out of wedlock, an unwanted child? What if they knew he was alive? What if they knew what he did for a living? What if it was they who paid for his schooling and the academy through that PO box? Had they been watching him from the shadows? Or maybe they thought he was dead. Maybe they had come looking for him and he hadn't been there. Maybe, just maybe.

He was eager to give them every benefit of the doubt if only he could meet them once, but what would he do then? What would he do with their presence in his life? There was a time when he had wanted to see them at any cost, but that desire had died long ago. Did he really want to see them anymore? He wasn't sure. He wasn't a normal guy living a normal life. He killed for a living. He risked his life. He dealt with the concept of death in real life, day in day out. What would he do with the two people about whom he had stopped caring eons ago?

For the next two weeks, he pondered over these questions. Should he go and look for them? There would be thousands of Laurens in the world. The number of US Presidents Albert might have seen probably hovered in double digits and he had no way to know which one Albert was talking about. Without a year or a specific duration, that part of the search was a non-starter. Albert was dead and buried. He wasn't coming back. Wick had no other source. For the next two weeks he sat in his room, thinking, analyzing, deciding.

.   .   .

Then the call came from his handler Riley, for this mission. At first, he'd said that he needed time but then he agreed. A diversion would do him good.


But sitting in that plane, he realized that he couldn't run from his own thoughts. He could not un-hear or un-see what he knew. He could do nothing to stop his mind from wandering into the dark bylanes of memory. He was still angry and he had no outlet for his anger.  Sitting in that plane, he was burning from within.

⊏⊐

"Landing in two minutes," the pilot announced on the radio.


"You ready?" Jessica touched Wick's shoulder softly and he jerked as if he had been in deep sleep. He nodded without looking at her and bent down to grab his bag from under the seat.


The aircraft descended, its flaps down, its powerful Rolls-Royce engines working to their maximum capacity, trying to stifle its speed all the way back. The tarmac at Vienna International Airport shone in the distance while the jet maneuvered for the touchdown. As soon as they landed, the countdown began.

# CHAPTER 7

A NONDESCRIPT MINIVAN waited for them outside the airport. Jakob, the TF-77's asset in Vienna, was driving. He didn't need any instructions, he knew where he had to take them. The minivan navigated the city traffic expertly, never going above the prescribed speed limit. No one stopped it. No one tailed it. But Jakob continued to take random turns and drove through the back alleys as a precaution. Inside the van, Wick and Stan were peering at Mac's laptop screen. Blueprints of the Venezuela consulate were spread across it. Mac had uploaded the copies of the blueprints on his and Jessica's laptop just before leaving. They had gone over them during the flight. Wick and Stan heard what they had to say and occasionally asked questions about stairs, exit doors, back channels, size of the rooms. Mac, and sometimes Jessica, responded to their queries. Once they were satisfied, Wick asked Mac to move to the names and profiles of the people who had landed in Vienna from Venezuela in the last forty-eight hours. The list had seventy-two people on it.

.  .  .

"Can you remove the names of people older than forty and younger than eighteen?" Wick asked.

Mac put the filters, and the number came down to thirty-seven.

"Can you triangulate their locations using their cell numbers given in their profiles?"

"It will take some time," Mac said.

"Okay."

"If you could tell me what it is you are looking for, I could help better," Mac said, hesitantly.

"People who are here for business or pleasure should be easily trackable, but the ones with off-the-grid phones, they are possibly the ones using a burner cell or a sat phone. We need to have those faces and names."

Mac nodded, trying not to look stupid and embarrassed. It was common sense and he should have applied that logic himself. Sitting behind Wick, Stan smiled at Mac's flushed face. Mac noticed it and shrugged. Wick couldn't see Stan's reaction but he noticed Mac's. Said nothing. He opened his bag and took out the manila folder that had the photos and names of consulate employees.

"We are near the safe house, have you checked your bags under your seats?" Jakob said without turning back.

Wick took his bag out and checked it - new identities, passports, use-and-throw money cards, some cash, and clothes. Jessica, Mac, and Stan did the same. Weapons and their disguise they would find in the safehouse.

Their covers were airtight. Wick was an IT contractor from London, Jessica was a journalist from Spain, Stan was on a business trip and Mac was an Audi salesman here to attend a sales retreat.

Carlos' meeting was the next morning and their plan was to leave for the consulate at dawn. Wick had already decided how to use that time. He knew that once he sneaked in the consulate, he might not even get time to breathe.

# CHAPTER 8

SAFE HOUSE, **Vienna**

Jakob dropped Wick and Mac at the safe house. Jessica and Stan had some other work, so they left with Jakob. The arrangement made Mac nervous. He didn't like being alone with Sam.

He was like a brick wall. Cold. Detached. Removed from his surroundings. Mac hated the fact that he could not get a read on him, like he could on Jessica, Stan or even McAvoy.

Wick didn't dally in the hall and went straight to the room assigned to him. A black oversized duffle bag was already on the bed. There was some food on a round coffee table along with a bottle of sparkling water. He went to the door and saw Mac fiddling with his computer. "You want to eat something?"

· · ·

"I already have mine in my room. What you got?" Mac responded instinctively and regretted it instantly.

"I don't know, you can check." Wick turned and walked back in. Mac reluctantly followed him.

Entering the room, Mac saw the bag open on the bed, revealing a veritable armory of dismantled weapons, numerous clips, and boxes of ammunition. He went to the table and briefly considered checking the food and then leaving, but then rejected the idea as overly rude. He ripped the cover open, leaned on the side table and began to eat.

Each one of them had a packed meal based on a form filled out by them long ago. It wasn't like they were asked to submit a form before every mission and despite Mac's efforts, he couldn't get his changed. It was a grouse that he carried everywhere. So it was a nice change to have something different. The second reason was that Mac saw this as a chance to get a foot in the door in understanding Wick. One's food tells a lot about oneself but based on Wick's palate, he resembled an innocent bank teller.

Wick stood near the bed, cleaning the first Beretta from the bag. He paused to take a deep swig from the bottle of water. Once done, Wick pulled back the slide, studied the gun with a keen eye, released it, carefully loaded a clip with bullets, and slid it into the pistol. Locked and loaded.

. . .

From a small wooden case, he selected a silencer that he screwed onto the gun. He set it down next to a pump action sawed-off shotgun, a sniper rifle, an old school Uzi submachine gun – silenced – with a polished mahogany stock, a K-Bar knife, and another Beretta.

"Did you get anything?" he suddenly uttered without looking at Mac.

Mac had his mouth full when he caught the question. He coughed twice in a bid to respond. Wick handed him an unopened water bottle and waited for him to catch his breath.

"I have found ten names who we might find in the consulate."

"Why these ten?"

"Their background checks have thrown some interesting anomalies." Wick was listening, so Mac continued "Somewhere in their timeline, there is a blip. For some years, they literally dropped off the grid as if they were dead or abducted by aliens." Mac tried injecting some humor, Wick responded with a mere nod, so Mac continued grudgingly, "... and then they resurfaced again with the same first name but a different last name."

Wick agreed with Mac's assessment. He knew even the best operatives had a hard time leaving their first names behind when they went for a new identity.

"How long will it take to vet the rest?"

"Couple of hours, maybe. It could be sooner if I get some alone time."

"Okay," Wick said and turned back to the open bag.

Instead of returning to his unfinished meal, Mac decided to ask Wick the question that was bothering him. He coughed to draw his attention. Wick looked at him.

"What is the plan?"

"Still a work in progress, but it will involve us joining the regular consulate cleaning crew."

"You mean you and Stan, right?"

Wick nodded.

What about Jessica?" Mac asked his next.

.  .  .

"She will be a part of the consulate's security detail, since we expect to find people in double digits as you have just mentioned, and we don't know what they are planning to do with Carlos. There will be civilians and diplomats too, so it's an all hands on deck kind of situation."

"What if they kill Carlos before we can get him out?"

"They won't, but if they do, we'll try to get his body out, or anything that would be of relevance."

"You're going into a high-security government building without a concrete plan?"

"I'm working on it. You'll be the first to know once it's ready," Wick said, without irritation or sarcasm, but also without a smile.

Mac asked nothing further. He finished his meal and fed the leftovers to the bin. He got up and walked towards the door. Wick's back was toward him.

"Don't worry, I'm not going to get your friends killed in the field," Wick said without turning back.

Mac stopped in his tracks, not knowing how to respond. He articulated a weak "Sure thing," and beat a hasty retreat.

# CHAPTER 9

SAFE HOUSE, **Vienna**

Jessica and Stan arrived two hours later. Mac was in the hall trying to get into the consulate's mainframe server.

"Where's Wick?" Jessica asked

"I think he went for a run," Mac said without looking at them.

"He told you that?" Stan said

"His outfit did," Mac responded sarcastically.

"Great, so now we can gossip about him." Stan smiled.

Mac gave a fake laugh.

"I thought you liked gossip," Stan said.

"I do, but not when I am trying to create a backdoor in a highly secured server."

"But thank God you both are still alive." Stan was not going to let Mac off the hook so easily.

"What do you mean?"

"Nothing." Stan grinned innocently.

"You definitely meant something, and you are going to tell me NOW," Mac said getting up from his chair.

Stan raised his hands defensively. "All I meant is that you don't seem to like him very much."

"He doesn't like the fact that he cannot get a read on him," Jessica said.

"Is that so, Mac?" Stan gave a smirk.

.  .  .

"I have no issues with him and if your mom can tolerate you, I'm sure I can work with him," Mac retorted.

"Don't bring my mom into this." Stan's smirk was gone.

"Well, she did bring you into this world without asking anyone," Mac smiled defiantly.

Stan stepped closer to him.

"Stop it guys," Jessica yelled, waving them both down. "Mac, you focus on your work, and Stan, I think it's time for you to call your mom and tell her that you've arrived safely," Jessica paused for a moment and then she and Mac burst out laughing.

"Et Tu, Jessica!" Stan protested.

"Well, it's funny that big Stan still lives with his mom," Mac said.

"She needs me."

"Is that the reason none of your girlfriends stay for more than three months?" Mac needled him.

.   .   .

"No, that's because of this job. But how would a thirty-year-old virgin nerd like you understand that?" Stan was back in the game.

"I am more manly than you ever will be."

"You are so manly they will cut off your dick and keep it in some museum for generations to see and that will be your legacy; probably your only one."

This time even Jessica smiled.

"It's no use talking to you," Mac said turning back to his laptop.

"On a serious note, Mac, have you seen anything strange in Wick's behavior?" Jessica asked.

"You mean the grumpy daddy behavior he threw at us during the trip? No, I didn't."

"I am serious."

.   .   .

"I don't know, Jessica, I'm working with him for the first time and it appears to me that all the stories about him are a figment of someone's imagination. He seems like any other agent to me - grumpy and full of himself. You've worked with him earlier. What do you think? Is he really that good?" Mac asked. Stan also eyed Jessica. This was important to him, "In one sentence, if I have to take only one person with me into any battle, it will be him." she stated.

"That good, eh? Hmmm... now, I am fine with this assessment, but I guess Stan is hurt. He really hoped that at the end of that sentence, you would take his name." Mac smirked at Stan. Stan made a face.

"Seriously, is he really that good?" Stan asked Jessica.

"There are many good agents, perhaps even better than him, and I have worked with most of them, but in a battlefield where even the best agents sometimes freeze, Wick consistently picks the right moves ninety-nine out of a hundred times. That can be the difference between life and death. His decision-making ability under extreme pressure is exceptional. With him on our side this might be the easiest assignment for us this year."

"I am impressed," Mac said. "Not by him, but by the way you talk about him. You guys aren't dating or something, are you?"

"Yeah, sure!" Jessica glared at Mac who sheepishly avoided her look.

# CHAPTER 10

WICK WALKED four blocks from the safe house and then took a cab to Sankt Elisabeth-Platz street. A DSLR camera hung around his neck, his fake passport was in his back pocket, a Nike cap, Ray-Ban aviators along with a t-shirt and a pair of jeans completed his tourist getup. The outing was a routine he preferred to follow on his every mission—to visually soak in the details of the location in advance and mark out possible roadblocks.

The cab dropped him near the Wieden Elisabeth Church at St. Elizabeth Square on Sankt-Elisabeth-Platz Street. He waited for it to leave before moving forward. The driver turned left towards Viktorgasse and Wick started to walk towards the Schloss Belvedere. The Belvedere was on the Prinz Eugenstraße. It was a historic building complex with two baroque palaces. Acres of green lent it a peaceful air. The grounds were set on a gentle gradient and included decorative tiered fountains and cascades, ornate sculptures, and majestic wrought-iron gates. Wick's interest, however, was in a building opposite the Belvedere grounds, but on the same street—the Venezuela consulate.

Wick walked past the embassy, casually checking the locations of the closed-circuit TV cameras. There were five—two covered the Belvedere garden view and the remaining three covered the street. One, in particular, was focused at the opening of the consulate. Wick steered clear of all five, keeping his head down.

The consulate building had four floors with parking at the front. Taking into account the building blueprints, he could imagine pipes and wires running through the concrete walls. The streets were packed with vehicles, but the consulate's entry space was deserted. The building to the right of the consulate housed an Asian spa and the one on the left had an AVK shopping store along with a software company called VIATEC. Wick had an interview scheduled in a day's time at VIATEC's office. In all probability he would not attend it, but it provided a great cover.

Playing the part of a tourist, Wick took a few photographs of the Belvedere greens. It was five in the evening, and no one gave him a second look. He strolled leisurely down the adjacent streets and thirty minutes later he ambled towards the Viktor Frankl Institute for Logotherapy and Existential Analysis from where he hitched a ride back to the same location four blocks away from the safe house, from where he had taken the earlier cab. He had some pointers that he wanted Mac to run through the system.

# CHAPTER 11

At eight that night, five people stood around the large table in the hall— Jessica, Mac, Stan, Jakob, and Wick. On the table, were pictures of sixteen people that Mac had identified as possible targets.

Wick picked up the photograph of the man with the scar. He was the one commanding these men tomorrow. Despite being in this field for a long time, he was a relatively unknown figure to the U.S. agencies. There wasn't much known about him and that worried Wick. If nothing else went his way, and if he killed only one man tomorrow, then it had to be him.

"This is your entry point." Jessica tapped the blueprint with her index finger. "Stan and Wick will replace these two from the morning cleaning crew ." She pointed to two photos. "I will replace him in the security team." She held up the third picture. "Mac has just injected a tiny virus into Vienna transport authority's master server that manages the traffic light system. Once we get out of the consulate, Mac will help Jakob to navigate the traffic by creating diversions for any trailing cars." She gestured at Wick to continue.

"They are not expecting anything surprising to go down tomorrow. Use silencers. Hand-to-hand combat is preferable to guns wherever possible. Our bags will be in the first floor janitorial room in the consulate." He looked at Jakob who nodded. It was his job. "Our priority is to find the target's location, his condition —dead or alive—and how fast we can extract him. I will lead. Stan will back me up." Wick paused for any questions. There were a couple.

"What about the exit plan?" Stan asked first.

"Wick has given me some pointers. I'm working on them." Mac responded this time. He was talking about Wick's visit to the consulate as a tourist.

"What about the civilians?" Stan asked.

"Avoid it but if not then go for a flesh wound," Jessica said.

.   .   .

"The shift changes at seven in the morning and then every eight hours," Wick said, referring to the working shifts in the consulate. "We will leave at five-thirty in the morning, so we need to be up at three-thirty. Get some sleep and be ready. Jakob, you will stay with us here tonight."

Jakob, Stan, and Jessica nodded. Mac looked at his laptop. The program was still running. The timer hovered at two hours and forty-two minutes. He still needed time to get into the consulate server. He decided to stay put.

# CHAPTER 12

CARLOS DISCONNECTED the call and looked at Karina, who was waiting for him near the fireplace. A portable wrought iron fire kettle hung over it. Outside, the sky was draped in bright stars. The temperature had been falling for the last three or four days, but the cabin was snug and comfortable.

He was dressed casually in a pair of jeans and a beat-up sweat-shirt. His old leather jacket hung on the armchair. He smiled at his fiancée but got nothing in return. She had just finished reading the final draft of his latest article which again lambasted the Venezuela government policies and the exasperation was visible on her face.

"When?" she asked about the publishing date, putting the papers on the table.

"Saturday," Carlos said.

.  .  .

"This Saturday?"

"Yes."

"On our wedding day?"

Carlos, with an impish grin and a beer in each hand, moved closer to her. Karina had to smile at his childish behavior. He kissed her on the lips.

"Can't it wait till the next week?" she asked.

"I thought you liked me for my tenacity," he replied.

Karina straightened up and took the beer from him. "Fine." She turned to the nearest chair. "Thanks for this." She signaled at the bottle.

Carlos smiled. That was easy, he thought. "You should relax and think about how we should celebrate tomorrow once we have the signed papers in our hands."

.  .  .

"Do you think it's wise to go into the consulate alone?" Karina asked, her tone laced with concern.

"Sweetie, this is Vienna, not Venezuela. Everything will be fine tomorrow. Just like the last time," Carlos assured her for the hundredth time in the same tone he had always used for this subject. This was probably the last time he was going to visit a place that was under the jurisdiction of his home country. Inside, he was equally worried about his appointment. All he wanted was that signed paper legalizing his status as a free man. A minor bit to begin his new life.

"I know," Karina said and rested her head on his chest.

"Good." Carlos gave her a long kiss on her forehead. He was head over heels in love with this woman. After a while, he worked his way to her ear and asked suggestively, "Shall we go upstairs now?"

"This place is as good as any," Karina whispered, seductively. He smiled and lifted her in his arms and lay her gently on the carpet near the fire. A fleeting thought about the coming day crossed his mind, but he discarded it. It was just a trivial signature.

# CHAPTER 13

THE FLOOR WAS hard and cold, yet the man rested peacefully on it. Through his naked back, the cold seeped into his body. Still only in his mid-thirties, his life had been incredibly hard. The abundance of scars on his body made him resemble a sculpture shaped by an angry creator. Every scar had a story, and at the end of those stories there were dead bodies. He could hide them all, except the one on his face. It had been given to him by an American, and he had hated them ever since.

The man was a Moroccan by birth, but he no longer claimed that part of his ancestry. He had taken to Christianity when he was fifteen because his own God had given him nothing but poverty and oppression. So, he sacked him and found a new one. The men who had introduced him to this new God also gave him a new name—Joaquin Thomas. They gave him food to eat and money to spend and a new nation to call his home—Venezuela. What he didn't know was that the food and that small change would cost him his innocence. Joaquin was in fact picked by a team of specialists. His life was now theirs and they could steer him any direction they wanted and steer they did. He joined the Venezuela Army at the age of eighteen and then moved up the ranks until he found himself in a team that reported directly to the director of the Venezuela's national intelligence agency.

His first assignment was to get Oscar Luis Cartaya out from the Volkel Air Base, a military base in the Netherlands. Oscar had been imprisoned twice by the government of Netherlands on the order of a Dutch court. According to Venezuela, Oscar was a retired Venezuelan general and former head of military intelligence, but the Dutch court believed he was one of the original members of La Fraternidad, a fringe group responsible for multiple homicides in the Netherlands, according to a report by the General Intelligence and Security Service, the Netherlands' secret service.

Once the court's decision came out, it provoked massive outrage in Venezuela, which responded aggressively to the arrest by calling the detention a "kidnapping" and sending its naval vessels. Instead of bowing before the pressure, the Netherlands went to the United Nations. To end the ensuing stalemate, Venezuela's national intelligence agency decided to send a team to free Oscar, but the mission bombed. In the attempt to free Oscar, Joaquin and the other men were captured and implicated on multiple charges. Joaquin, along with the others, was tortured for a year. They all broke eventually. Some were willing to say anything to be free of the pain, yet succumbed to it eventually. Others spoke the truth and still perished. The lucky few were those who died the earliest and were thus spared the extended agony and humiliation. Joaquin saw everything and survived everything, and it brought him closer to his God.

Finally, he was among the few survivors who managed to return to Venezuela as part of a prisoner exchange program. By not telling his captors about his bosses, he gained a reputation in Venezuela's secret service group. The torture, the hardship, the suffering—it was all worth it. For once he got hold of a rope of his own, he rose quickly within the organization.

Soon he became the de facto asset for anything that needed to be done precisely and quietly. Henrique had told him in private that this would be his last mission in the field. They were planning to swear him in as the second-in-command in the Venezuela Intelligence Service.

It was a position he had been eyeing for a long time, and in less than twelve hours, it would be within his grasp.

# CHAPTER 14

0525 HOURS, **Safehouse**

Jakob switched on the ignition of the minivan at 0520. He didn't have to wait long. At exactly 0530 the gate of the safe house opened, and four silhouettes walked towards the vehicle in the pre-dawn gloom.

"Good morning," Jakob greeted the team.

"Morning, Jakob," Jessica responded, getting into the front passenger seat beside him, as Stan and Mac took the middle row, leaving the third row to Wick.

Jakob hit the accelerator, and the tires whirred on the road. Wick sat in silence, his eyes closed. It was a ritual he followed before every mission, visualizing the location and the faces of the people he would encounter on the mission.

The consulate was more than an hour away in normal city traffic. So early in the morning, though, they were able to make good time. Jakob's familiarity with secluded alleyways and insider knowledge of the streets was unbeatable. Despite not taking the straight route to the consulate, they were standing at their first designated stop, at the Viktor Frankl Institute on the Prinz Eugen-Straße at seven past six. Wick and Stan got out of the minivan and started to walk towards the consulate building. Jakob drove on with Jessica and Mac. He dropped Jessica at the second stop- Wist Walter GesmbH, which was a shoe repair shop four blocks away from the consulate. Then he and Mac proceeded to the Cafe Goldegg that was two blocks away from the embassy.

All this while Mac was drinking a Red Bull. He had not slept at all and this was the only way to keep him awake. He had been able to crack the system only a couple of hours ago. They now had a backdoor bypassing the server encryption. The malware was now in the system waiting for the reboot. Based on the daily security protocol of the consulate, the security admin would start the reboot of the mainframe server at six-thirty every morning. Once the system restarted, the malware would be uploaded giving Mac parallel control of the security system for the whole building —the closed-circuit TV cameras, fire alarms and everything else connected to it.

.   .   .

He checked the signal and was comforted to see that their proximity was good enough for him to be ready when the system rebooted. As soon as he got the access, his first job would be to get Wick's, Stan's, and Jessica's the identification data plugged into the embassy's system. The only thing he had to do now was wait.

# CHAPTER 15

At the back door entry where the embassy crew entered, Wick swiped his card. The man sitting behind the system looked at his face and then back to the screen. He waited a couple of seconds and then signaled him to move forward. Stan was seventh in line. The same routine was followed, and he was in the building. At the front door, Jessica checked in with her ID card. The process went smoothly for her too. At Mac's computer screens, he saw them moving along with the others and heaved a sigh of relief. The first hurdle was crossed without anyone raising any alarm.

Stan and Wick walked with the rest of the crowd, following the building supervisor towards the janitorial room. Stan was right behind the supervisor, while Wick was at the back, keeping a suitable distance from Stan and letting others fill the gap between them. From the corner of his eye, Wick perused the

CCTV cameras to his right while Stan took care of those on the left. They needed to protect their covers more than anything else. Not making eye contact with the others was the most basic thing they could do apart from a confident gait. The longer that illusion remained, the higher the chances of their plans working.

Once inside the janitor's room, the supervisor mechanically read the locations from a sheet of paper, specifying where each of his men would be for the next eight hours. Stan was assigned to the third-floor bathroom while Wick got the guest lounge on the first floor.

Once he finished, everyone began to put on their uniforms. Wick and Stan followed suit, but a trifle slow. Standing at the opposite corners and away from the entry door, they were observing everything with neutral expressions. The manager glanced at the two new recruits. He had received their details in the morning roster. The temp agency filled in the positions whenever anyone was on leave or dropped off the grid. He didn't need to call them. It was the agency's job to get their verification and get their records fed into the Consulate's database. He was pleased as long as the overall count remained the same. What he didn't know was that today was different. Stan and Wick's records were entered into the system by Mac and the temps on leave would still be getting their wages for the day. The agency would not have had any information about two of its temps not reporting for work. It was a complex web of redirected email communication regulated by Mac's computer.

.   .   .

Before leaving the room, the supervisor walked to Wick, "Any questions?"

"No, sir," Wick replied, with brief eye contact.

The supervisor then asked Stan the same question. He shook his head and he seemed satisfied.

"Don't forget your walkies," the supervisor said to everyone in general as he was leaving the room. Wick checked the device, switched it on. Listened momentarily to the sound of static, then turned it off. It was a rudimentary Motorola device and he didn't intend to use it, but he clipped it to his belt as instructed. Gradually the crowd started thinning. The supervisor was gone, and no one looked back to check on the others in the room. It was a tedious job and they all were going to be at their places until they were told otherwise.

A few minutes later, Stan and Wick were the only ones in the room. The door clicked shut, and their relaxed bodies immediately stiffened. Stan turned and moved a big cardboard box at his left, revealing the same bag that Wick had in the safe house. He grabbed it and put it on the floor. Wick crouched and unzipped the bag, grabbing two Berettas from the top. The magazines and K-Bar knife followed. Stan took out his SIG Sauer P320, three magazines, and a military grade knife. They left rest of the ammo in the bag and put it back to its place. Once they were both ready with the weapons concealed underneath their loose uniforms, they picked up military-grade Bluetooth earpieces and inserted them in their ears.

"Sam Wick checking in. Over."

"Stan checking in. Over."

"Jessica checking in. Over."

"Mac checking in. Over."

# CHAPTER 16

Stan proceeded to the third-floor bathroom. Memorizing the building plans helped him to create a mental layout of the floor. While taking the elevator, he saw Jessica manning the entry gate as part of the security.

Wick remained on the first floor, ambling towards the guest lounge. He identified a vantage point to keep an eye at the main entrance. The footfall in the lobby had begun to grow. People were beginning to trickle through the security gate on their way to work. Wick roughly counted the number of personnel on his floor.

The Ambassador was not in yet. The wooden door of his office was being guarded by two officers to prevent any unauthorized entry.

. . .

"Hi, I need an air freshener in my office." It was a female voice behind him. He turned around and saw a tall brunette standing outside an office. She was looking straight at him. "Excuse me, can you bring an air freshener?" she repeated.

"Yes, ma'am." Wick walked back towards the janitor room and found the air freshener bottle at the top of the second shelf from the door. Minutes later he was standing outside the woman's office, checking the nameplate on the door: Ana Sofía, Minister-Counselor.

"Can you use it in there?" Ana indicated the space behind a large steel cupboard. Wick pressed the nozzle and sprayed it behind and around the cupboard.

Ana took a deep breath checking the odor. "Thank you, I think that will do," she said.

Wick nodded politely and left the office, closing the door behind him.

He then heard Jessica's voice in his earpiece, "He's here."

He walked swiftly towards the pre-decided vantage point to see the reception area. The man with the scar and Felipe were walking towards the Ambassador's office. There were two more men behind them. Wick recognized them from the photos. The door to the ambassador's office opened, and all four disappeared inside.

# CHAPTER 17

"Get ready." Joaquin was in the CCTV control room along with Felipe and the Ambassador.

His men had already taken positions on the second, third and fourth floors. They all had their sat phones switched on, waiting for their orders from their boss, Joaquín.

Carpio wasn't too happy with the way these men had taken over his turf, men who normally would have no standing in the embassy. These people were merely hitmen. He was a respected diplomat, tempted to assert his authority, but at the last moment, he bit his lower lip and stopped himself from saying anything he might regret later. He swallowed his pride and stood quietly at one side while Joaquin and Felipe studied the CCTV footage. Suddenly, there was some movement on one of the screens and the two men straightened their backs, their eyes shining with glee.

Carlos Cruz had just gotten out of a Fiat outside the building. Joaquin studied him with a smile, as Felipe alerted their men to get ready. Their prey had arrived.

The job was simple, yet the consequences would be unimaginable if anything went wrong. The diktat from Henrique was clear —bag and tag with minimum hassle.

In the CCTV control room, the three pairs of eyes were watching the live feed of the entry on the screens. Carpio's throat felt parched. He had no idea what Joaquin and his men intended for Carlos, but he knew it wasn't going to be a friendly chat.

Joaquin and Felipe exchanged confident looks. They expected things to go down smoothly from here. Their evening flight back to Venezuela was already booked. Joaquín's last mission was going to be the shortest and the easiest.

At the checkpoint, Carlos was asked to remove his belt and shoes for the metal detector. He glanced up at the CCTV camera pointed at him. In the control room, Joaquin's eyes met Carlos's.

# CHAPTER 18

CARPIO'S FOREHEAD glistened with sweat. As soon as Carlos crossed the first threshold, Carpio realized that either way he was screwed. This was the end of his political career. Anything that happened to this man on his watch would effectively mean that this would be his last rodeo as a politician. Unofficially, it was like being asked to retire from active politics. He had played the scenarios numerous times in his head. And in none of the outcomes did he come out unscathed. From the time the telephone on his desk had rung, he was doomed. Henrique, the Venezuela intelligence service director, was clear in his instructions to Carpio as to what was expected of him, and that when the job was underway, he would need to take a step back. As Carlos walked into the embassy the reality of all of this happening hit the Ambassador with the force of a truck and he slumped on the chair behind him.

Joaquin turned around to look at him. The ambassador was looking pale.

. . .

"Handle yourself. We don't have time to babysit you," Joaquin ordered him in a stern voice. He knew the strength and repercussions of even minor nagging doubts in people. Every job's success lay in all its pieces moving in tandem, like a symphony. Any feelings not aligned with the task tended to manifest into actions at exactly the wrong moment, derailing the momentum and snowballing body count.

"What are you going to do with him?" Carpio asked

"The less you know, the better. Hand me your ID card."

"Why?" Carpio demanded shakily.

Joaquin looked at Felipe and tilted his chin towards Carpio. Felipe grabbed the handles of Carpio's chair, startling him. "If you ask one more stupid question, I will cut you to pieces. You understand?" Carpio nodded in fear and unwillingly took out his ID card. Felipe let go of the chair.

"It's time to get everyone out of the building," Joaquin said. "Tell everyone in the consulate that they need to leave after fifteen minutes, not before. We don't want Carlos to notice anything abnormal."

"What about Ana?" Carpio was worried about her. He hadn't had time to explain the situation to her.

. . .

"Let the girl stay. Carlos met her last time, so we need her to welcome him and bring him to your office without any glitch."

"But...." Carpio wanted to say something, but a stare from Felipe was enough to seal his mouth.

"Now leave. We will be watching your every move. Don't fuck up." Carpio got up and walked out. In his office, he picked up the phone. His first call was to Ana. He instructed her to receive Carlos and bring him to his office. His second and third calls were to the security and building supervisors with specific instructions given to him by Joaquin.

# CHAPTER 19

"HELLO, CARLOS." Ana greeted him with a smile and an extended hand.

"Hi, Ana." He shook her hand.

"Your papers are ready. I will get them to you in a minute."

"Any other formalities?"

"Yeah, a couple, but it won't take more than a couple of hours."

"I was hoping it would be quicker," Carlos sighed, not too happy at the prospect of having to wait among those whose loyalty lay with the regime.

.  .  .

"A couple of hours is very fast, compared to getting a signature in Venezuela." She gave him a magnetic smile. "But if you don't want to wait, you can come back at 1:00 p.m."

"It's okay, I will wait here." Carlos didn't want to appear rude to Ana whom he thought highly of since their meeting the previous week. She was the one who had taken care of his documents, which otherwise could have taken months to get approved.

"Oh, and I forgot to mention, Carpio wants to meet you," Ana said.

"The Ambassador?"

"Yes. I think he was in a meeting last time when you were here."

"Anything important?" Carlos didn't want to sound rude since he still needed the signed documents, but he was wary of the Ambassador's agenda.

"I don't think so. More like an informal meeting, I would say."

"Okay," Carlos said, straightening his jacket as he followed her. He braced himself mentally, knowing the only possible agenda the Ambassador could want to discuss was his hardline approach towards Venezuela and its President in his columns.

.   .   .

For no particular reason, Carlos recollected his first column for which he had received a phone threat. In that column for the NY Times, Carlos had written about how he feared being arrested in a clear crackdown on dissent overseen by the President since his re-election. He had related the stories of people who had been arrested, even without being dissidents, just for the crime of having an independent mind. It was that article that had raised his profile in the circuit. Since then, he had written numerous articles. Getting death threats was a professional hazard of his chosen brand of voice and he was now used to them.

Today, however, he felt a distinct sense of unease. He would be facing not an anonymous caller on the other end of a phone line, but someone who was a direct representative of the President in Vienna. However, Carlos knew he didn't have to say anything or agree to anything. He was in a neutral country, after all, and there was nothing the Ambassador could do to make him comply. He just had to stay quiet and bide his time. Controlling his anger was crucial. At most he would receive a slap on the wrist, nothing more.

He couldn't have been more wrong.

# CHAPTER 20

THE LARGE WOODEN door separating the waiting lounge and the ambassador's office opened and Carlos saw the coat of arms of his nation engraved on the wall behind the plush chair of the ambassador. Ana escorted him inside the room. He shook hands with the ambassador, faking a polite smile.

"Ana, why don't you go and get his documents," Carpio said with a nervous smile.

"Sure," Ana said and left the room, leaving him and Carlos alone.

"Please have a seat." Carpio offered Carlos while sitting himself.

"Thank you, Mr. Ambassador."

. . .

"Please call me Carpio. What would you like to have? Tea, coffee, anything else?"

"Just the papers." His tone betrayed a hint of irritation.

"Sure. Ana is working on it, and I believe she had already told you how long it will take."

"Yeah, she has. What did you want to discuss?"

"First, let me order coffee for you." He picked up the phone and ordered two coffees. Carlos said nothing. It was just coffee. He gave another obligatory smile to Carpio.

Five minutes later the door opened, and he heard two sets of footsteps behind him. Carlos looked at Carpio, who was looking at the two new entrants. One of them came up and dragged a chair next to Carlos, while the second one stood right behind him.

"Hello, Carlos." Joaquin gave a cold smile.

Carlos felt as if he had skipped a beat. This was a nightmare and he just needed to wake up to get out of this.

.   .   .

"Glad you haven't forgotten me."

# CHAPTER 21

ANA REALIZED something wasn't right as soon as she pushed the door open. Carpio looked at her in confusion. The phone receiver was in his hand and the phone ringing on the other side sat in Ana's office. Carpio had been calling to tell her to stay in her office, but he had obviously been too late. He looked at the two men and Ana with uncertainty. Ana looked at Carlos and saw fear in his eyes. The man sitting beside him was the one she had seen the previous morning. She hadn't liked him then, and she didn't like him now. His face had a menacing look, unlike anything she had ever seen.

"What's happening?" she asked in a high pitch.

"Ana, go home," Carpio said, hastily.

"Who are these people?" She demanded.

. . .

"Didn't you hear him? Get out." Joaquin spoke this time, his tone impatient.

"Who are these people?" She ignored Joaquin and addressed her boss.

"None of your business, now get lost." Joaquin was getting angry. The one thing he could never tolerate was disobedience in a woman.

"I am not talking to you," Ana shouted back. "Carpio, what is going on?"

Joaquin looked at Felipe.

"I will tell you who are we." Felipe, who was standing behind Carlos, suddenly took a menacing step towards her. She took a step back while looking at Carpio, expecting him to intervene. Instead, she found a defeated man, who avoided her eyes.

Felipe grabbed her wrist and Ana was stunned for a moment to think that something like this was happening to her in her office. She recovered quickly and, with a swift jerk, she drew herself away from Felipe's grip. "Keep your bloody hands off me."

. . .

Felipe, somewhat surprised at this unexpected show of strength, paused momentarily and then swung his hand at her, palm open. Ana saw the blow coming and instinctively raised her arm to protect herself, but it still knocked her off balance. Her resistance amplified Joaquin's rage. He got up and strode to her. Once close, he swung a punch at her stomach. It connected squarely and she crumpled to the floor, curling up in a small ball. He didn't stop there and kicked her. She screamed in pain.

Joaquin looked at Felipe who grabbed her by her hair and dragged her on the floor mercilessly, kicking and hitting her at the same time. On his sat phone, Joaquin yelled for someone to get in the office. Carpio heard men running in the passageway.

The door burst open and three men entered. Felipe released Ana's hair and she sank on the floor, lying there sobbing, her hands covering her face.

"Teach her how to be a woman, and then take care of her. She will go down the drain with Carlos today." Felipe said. The men smiled. Two of them grabbed Ana's hands and dragged her out of the office. Ana cried out for help, but she didn't know that the entire consulate had been vacated on her boss's orders. She was all alone at their mercy.

# CHAPTER 22

ONE OF THE men struck her again to keep her quiet, and she lost consciousness.

"You," the leader among the three said to one of the other two. "Carry her on your shoulder. We are taking her to the second floor." They glanced at each other with smirks on their faces.

At the second-floor restroom, they threw her to the floor. One of them splashed water on her face till she opened her eyes groggily. Even before she could comprehend what was happening, a pair of hands grabbed her by the shoulders. A second later she was on her feet, face-to-face with her assaulter. He forcefully planted a kiss on her lips. She recoiled in horror. The two men standing behind her pushed her towards the man who kissed her.

.  .  .

This time the man grabbed Ana by the throat and squeezed tightly. Ana flailed her arms desperately. Her eyes grew wider as her lungs craved for oxygen.

Darkness threatened her vision and in a frantic effort to break free she rammed her right leg up into her assailant's groin.

The man tumbled back, and she was free, coughing, massaging her neck. But her blurred vision prevented her from seeing the oncoming blow. It caught her squarely on her right temple. She spun in the air, screaming in pain.

# CHAPTER 23

WICK HEARD THE MUFFLED SCREAMS. The restrooms shared the same corner on each floor, with drain pipes running like a backbone within the walls. Although the sounds were faint, the pipes carried them to the floor below without interference. Wick knew what it could be, but he couldn't understand why an elite force would do something like this. What he forgot was that the hostiles were trained mercenaries and not soldiers like him.

When the embassy employees got the orders to vacate the embassy. Wick, Jessica, and Stan decided to hide on their respective floors. The decision to vacate the embassy had its pros and cons. On one hand, it meant that there would be no collateral damage and on the other, it meant that they now had to wait for their chances. Luckily, they had Mac stationed outside checking the CCTVs to let them know the enemy's position. The only places Mac did not have access to were the restrooms and janitor rooms, and the ambassador's private suite on the fourth floor.

.  .  .

"Mac, where's Carlos?" Wick asked.

"Carpio's office."

"What about the others?"

"The Ambassador is at his chair. The man with the scar is talking to someone on the phone. Felipe is at the door."

"Did you see a woman?"

"Yes, three men took one to the north wing's restroom on the second floor, right above your location."

"Armed?" Wick asked.

"Probably... why?" Mac had a sinking feeling in his stomach. "Sam, what are you thinking?" There was no response. Mac spoke urgently, "Sam, you must not compromise the mission. This..." He stopped. The static over the comms meant Sam had disconnected.

"Jessica... can you hear me?" Mac switched to Jessica.

.   .   .

"Yes."

"I think Sam is going to do something he shouldn't."

"What?"

Mac gave her a short version of what had just happened.

Jessica took a few seconds to revert to Mac with her update. "His radio is off, I cannot reach him. I'm on the second floor but it's not wise to go out now without knowing what Wick is thinking."

"Then let's hope he doesn't do anything stupid," Mac said with a sigh.

⊏⊐

Wick was still in the restroom, thinking. Saving the girl meant exposing himself and jeopardizing the mission. There was no point in introducing new complications into a job that was going smoothly. Their target was still alive, and they still had the element of surprise on their side.

He was contemplating his options when he heard the screams again and his brain revolted. They had left no other option for him but to act.

.  .  .

*Damn it*, he cursed under his breath.

He got up and walked to the door. Putting his right hand on the knob, he closed his eyes and pictured the layout of the first floor. Five steps to the left from the restroom were the stairs that went to the second floor. He rotated the knob anticlockwise and the door opened without making any sound. From the sliver between the door and the wood frame, he watched the lobby. It was deserted.

He opened the door and walked towards the stairs—fourteen steps to the second floor broken into two sets. He looked at the nearest CCTV camera.

Mac saw Wick's face on the screen and then watched him breaking into a run towards the second floor. Wick climbed the stairs without making any noises. He paused briefly at the second-floor restroom door, to steady his movement.

Watching him standing at the closed door made Mac sweat.

⊏━━⊐

Ana was on the bathroom floor. The man who had kissed her had pushed her down violently. She had no strength left to resist her captors. The man now offered her his hand. She had no choice but to take it. He helped her up. She was bleeding, her eyes moist. She tried to speak but no words came.

·  ·  ·

The man flicked open a knife. "No shouting," he said pressing the knife at her throat, opening a small cut. Ana groaned. He then used the blade to push her to her knees. With his other hand, he unzipped his pants and forced himself into her mouth. Ana used both her hands against his thighs to resist, but one of the two men standing behind her kicked her back. and she jerked forward. The third man behind Ana ripped her pants open, trying to enter her from behind.

Sitting in the minivan, Mac was glued to his screen, observing Wick's tense posture at the restroom's closed door. He didn't know what was going on behind that door. It was suicide for Wick to expose himself when the stage was so neatly set, but there was nothing he could do. Jessica and Stan were with him on the line, waiting to hear an update. Wick's choice had a direct impact on those two, but it was Mac who was sweating incessantly. Jakob, who was hearing everything too, came to the back of the van to sit beside Mac.

"What is he doing?" Jakob asked watching Wick.

"I hope not something stupid." Mac was angry and scared at the same time. "Sam, don't open that door, goddammit," he muttered under his breath.

Wick, unaware of all of this, took a deep breath and turned the doorknob.

. . .

The commotion inside paused as the door clicked open. Wick took in the whole scene at a glance. On his screen, Mac could see the same woman he had seen earlier, on her knees on the washroom floor. The rest of his view was blocked by Sam.

Wick recognized the woman. She was the one who had asked for the air freshener. Three men standing, two with their pants down. Her clothes— torn. Her eyes—teary. Her hair— disheveled. Ana looked at Wick with hope but then she recognized him. He was the one from the cleaning crew, not someone who would stick his neck out for her.

What was he doing here when everyone was gone?

The three men gazed at him, shocked and worried. They now had two witnesses, both alive.

To Wick, the three men looked similar. Olive skin, lean muscular builds, dirty complexions, same insignia branded on their right wrists—a flying eagle forged from their burnt skin. Wick saw two Glock-26 and three satphones, out in the open – resting on the sink top and the floor, out of immediate reach of their owners.

His mind raced to capture and evaluate his surroundings. His position, the position of the girl, and of each of the three men. His pulse racing, Wick swung the door shut. The two men moved to get their pants back up in momentary confusion.

.   .   .

No one spoke.

Wick's face had contorted into a menacing look. His eyes narrowed, his jaw clenched, and beads of sweat appeared on his forehead.

"Who are you?" The one man with his pants still on strode towards Wick waving the Glock-26 at his face. His skull shone through his cropped hair, a scar mark on his neck. Wick could make out a combat vest under his Nike t-shirt. The man had not made up his mind to shoot Wick. It was not his decision to make, but that of his boss, Joaquin. But Wick had decided. A series of frozen pictures flashed through his head as his brain calculated and analyzed a thousand details in a millisecond. Unimportant parts of the room faded away—walls, doors, furniture, faces—leaving only what was necessary.

The clean rectangular glass plate above the basin. The scar covering the carotid on the neck of the man, walking towards him, gun in hand. The throbbing heartbeat at the center of the second man's chest. The loose steel soap dispenser cap on the edge of the sink near the second man. The second man's eye, and his gun that was thirty feet away from his right hand. The pointed barrette in Ana's disheveled hair.

Weapons, and for each weapon, the intended target—everything disconnected from any sense of humanity. He calculated the distance between each object and the time it would take him to hit his mark.

.   .   .

Then everything happened in the blink of an eye. For everyone in the room, the three things that transpired defied any explanation. There was no form or grace to it, just brutal efficiency.

Wick hit the glass shelf with the edge of his right palm, snapping it in two. He grabbed one half of the jagged glass edge. It hissed through the air and entered the man approaching Wick, revisiting the scar mark on his neck, leaving an opera of blood in the air. The two men gasped and fumbled in their attempt to get their pants back up and took a step back from the girl. The leader of the two dived for his Glock, but Wick was already moving across the bathroom bypassing Ana who was still on the floor, shocked and now blood-soaked. Wick's left hand swept across her hair, grabbing her barrette. Ana's head was yanked back, and she fell on her back. The clip changed hands and Wick planted the sharp angle of the clip deep into the eye of the diving man. The opponent lost his balance and his eye hit the ceramic pot, driving the barrette deep into his brain.

That was when the last man standing, seized his Glock from the sink top and jerked it in a sweeping motion from right to left. He was halfway into the sweep that should have ended with a bullet in his opponent when Wick scooped the soap dispenser cap from the bottle at the sink and rammed the steel pipe of the cap into his left eye socket. The man stopped midway, losing the Glock. He fell to the floor, quivering like a frog in a science experiment. The yelling started a second later, once the sensation of pain reached his brain, but Wick gagged his cries with a dusting cloth from his back pocket before they could turn dangerous. Then with his other hand he punched at his mouth to push the cloth further in. The blow hit his teeth hard and a couple of them fell inside his mouth. The man squirmed on the floor like a fish out of water. Both his hands covered his bleeding eye and lips, but the agony was unbearable.

Ana watched the quivering man with shock. The fear on his face was scary. The fact that she had just gone through a similar fear of death made her empathize momentarily with the man who had just tried raping her, but it didn't last long.

Wick knelt beside the man and grabbed his throat to steady him, watching Ana from the corner of his eye. She was shivering, but in control. He looked at the man and put a finger on his lips in a warning gesture. The outcome was immediate. The man used all his strength to gag his cries. He definitely wanted to live and no one except Wick could grant him that wish.

"I'm going to ask you a few questions. If you shout, I'll kill you. You understand?"

The man nodded. Once sure that the man wasn't lying, Wick loosened his grip on the man's throat and removed the cloth.

"What are you going to do with Carlos?"

. . .

The man didn't respond for a moment. Wick didn't have time to play. He gagged him again and punched him in the face, breaking three more teeth. Pain shot through the man's skull. His vision blurred. He tapped the floor furiously to let Wick know he would talk.

"Kill him," he said spluttering blood all over himself.

"Where?"

"Fourth floor. I don't know the room, but it has no cameras."

"Who is your leader?" Wick asked and the man hesitated this time. He shouldn't have because this time, after gagging him again, Wick rammed the back of his skull against the floor. The man's left hand relinquished his bleeding eye to grab his head, but Wick clutched his left wrist and put his knee on the other, killing his movements. The man squirmed to free himself, but Wick's grip made it impossible. He could not scream, he could not move.

Ana could not bear the bloodshed. It was brutal. She closed her eyes and used her hands to muffle her own screams.

"I won't ask again?" Wick bent to the level of the man's ear and whispered. The man nodded. Anything to lessen the pain.

.   .   .

"Joaquin Thomas."

"Keep on talking."

"We will cut his dead body into pieces and dissolve it in acid." The man was almost blabbering in fear. Ana gasped loudly. They were going to do the same with her. Wick looked at her and closed his eyes to signal silence.

"Where's the acid?"

"The minitruck with the container is yet to arrive."

"What's the license plate number?"

"I d...don't know."

"Where's it coming from?"

"I... I don't know."

"Who ordered the hit?"

.  .  .

"Henrique." He was talking about the director of the Venezuela Intelligence Service.

"The ambassador, is he also involved?" Wick asked his last question.

"Yes."

"Thank you." He pressed the cap into his eye socket with his left hand, driving it deep enough to pierce the man's brain. The man squirmed on the floor for a few seconds before he stopped moving.

Wick slowly got up, stepping back, gazing at the massacre around him. Heartbeats, the rush of blood, the sigh of breath - all ceased. The room was quiet. Ana was curled up in a corner. The natural order had been restored. His pent-up anger for his parents felt lighter. He looked at the dead bodies and jerked as if snapping back to reality.

He walked up to the sink and turned on the faucet, washing away the blood. He then looked up at his reflection in the mirror. It was a stranger staring back at him.

# CHAPTER 24

IN THE MIRROR, Wick observed Ana, she was still at the same place looking at him with fear. He closed his eyes. A sense of calmness wrapped him. The angst and the anger for his parents seemed to subsidize momentarily. He knelt, this time to sift through the pockets of the dead. Wallets, Glock magazines, lighter and some cash. He grabbed one of the sat phones, took out the ID cards from the wallets and discarded the rest. Once satisfied, he then looked at Ana. She was still on the floor, shivering.

He could understand. She had witnessed enough in the last few minutes to scar her for life.

"You okay?" He moved towards her. She pushed herself away from him, instinctively, but the wall behind limited her movement. Watching her, Wick paused.

.   .   .

"Ana, I will not hurt you, but we need to move quickly."

She looked at him and nodded. Wick reached down again, took her hand and gently helped her up. She didn't resist.

They had to move fast. The three dead men, when they won't report back, someone would come looking for them. No matter how optimistic anyone could be in that situation, it was bound to happen and when it did, they would know that they were not alone in the building.

"Why did they want to kill you?"

"I entered the Ambassador's office and I saw these two men threatening Carlos. When I objected and demanded who they were, this happened." Her sobs had subsided.

"Listen, I have to move and get you someplace where you'll be safe, more of them could come at any minute." He knew where he needed to take her. None of the rooms in the consulate would be safe when this was over, except the one place he knew no one would look. "Everything's gonna be alright," he assured her as he strode across the restroom and opened the janitor's closet. It was large enough for Ana to hide. He grabbed two white towels from the upper shelf and handed them to her. She took them without a word.

.   .   .

"Ana, stay here, someone will come back for you soon but till that time, you cannot come out. Whatever happens, make no sound. You understand me?" He spoke to her softly, but firmly.

She nodded.

Wick helped her inside the closet and made space for her on the floor.

"You have a cell phone?" he asked.

"No, I think I lost it somewhere in the struggle."

"Anything that could make a sound?"

She shook her head.

"Okay, I will close this door and it'll be dark in there, but you stay put. You got me?"

"Yes."

Wick closed the closet door and then looked at the three dead bodies. There was no use trying to hide them and clean the mess. The only thing he could hope for was that he would manage to get Carlos before the bodies were discovered.

# CHAPTER 25

ONCE ANA WAS SAFE, Wick switched on the comms. "Can you hear me?" Wick whispered over the static, careful to not let Ana hear anything.

"Affirmative," Jessica and Stan replied together. Mac responded soon after. They had all been waiting for this call.

"I hope that Mac has told you everything?"

Jessica and Stan hesitated before replying in affirmative. Mac stayed silent, he didn't know what to say.

"Then I will tell you what you don't know." Wick knew that Mac had no access to the inside of the restrooms. "I've got a survivor and three dead bodies in here."

.  .  .

"Who's the survivor? Are you hurt?"

"A consulate employee, I am fine, but we will need to speed up."

"Okay."

"Mac? What is the situation in the Ambassador's office?"

"They have just taken Carlos inside the elevator in Carpio's office."

"To where?"

"Possibly to the fourth floor, his private suite."

"Okay, tell me everything happening on the fourth floor. The number of hostiles, their weapons, their positions. Then repeat the same for the other floors," Wick said.

Mac described as asked. The fourth floor was isolated except for the south wing where two men manned the ambassador's suite. There was no camera in that room.

.   .   .

The third floor was a different story. There was an army of men. This is the floor where Stan was hiding. Mac counted eight, all armed, stationed in different rooms. He was in the middle of all this when all of a sudden, his screen went blank.

"Can you hear me, Stan? Wick?" Mac was thrown off the guard.

"Yes, we can. Everything good?"

"I think they've pulled the plug from the CCTV control room."

"Can you fix that?" Jessica asked.

"I don't think so unless someone goes there and manually plugs it in."

"What do you suggest?" Jessica spoke.

"We will wait. We already have a pretty good idea on the number of hostiles. Three dead. Eight men on the third floor. Two on the fourth and possibly two or three inside the suite with Carlos. Jessica sweep the first floor, especially the Ambassador's office. I will take care of the second. Stan, you stay put on third. We need to comb the first and second floor before we take on the third. Do not engage until fired at first and be wary of any traps."

·  ·  ·

"Got it." Stan and Jessica replied.

# CHAPTER 26

JESSICA WAS HOLED up inside a pantry room on the first floor. She opened the door slowly and peered outside. The floor was empty. From her squatted position, her eyes swept the area from the consulate's modest reception area to the guest lounge. The ambassador's office covered most of the real estate on the floor. There were two elevators on each floor that required a key card interlinked with the employee ID to enter. Any guest needed to be escorted by either a security personnel or an employee to use them. There was also an elevator in the ambassador's office for his exclusive use which opened to the private suite on the fourth floor. That was where Carlos was now. Access to the elevator was limited to the office bearer.

The rest of the space was dedicated to his secretary's office, a conference room and small pantry space. Each floor had two sets of restrooms, at opposite ends and perpendicular to the main entrance. Jessica checked her SIG Sauer P320 and then walked towards the restroom in the direction of Carpio's office. At the door, she stood silently, listening carefully for any sounds.

Her weapon was ready, in case of any confrontation, she had to be the first one pulling the trigger. From her place, the main conference room was to her left, and the Ambassador's personal assistant's office was to her right. Jessica decided to check the conference room first. It was vacant as she had expected. In the same squatted position, she next combed the vacant office of Carpio's PA. The SIG in her right hand was ready to be fired if needed. The last place left was the Ambassador's office. She moved to it in the crouched position. Her hand was on the door-knob, ready to turn it, when she heard the elevator inside the ambassador's office opening.

# CHAPTER 27

JESSICA QUICKLY RETREATED to the vacant PA's office slowly closing the door behind her. From her back pocket, she took out a micro-sized spy-cam attached with a foldable wire with a screen at the other end. It was tiny enough to pass through the gap between the floor and the wooded door. She carefully checked the lobby. On the screen she could see that it was still deserted, but there were murmurs. Someone was in Carpio's office.

The ambassador's office door opened, and Jessica quickly retracted the tiny cam. Sitting in the darkness, she could hear two distinct voices in the hallway.

"You don't get it, you can't kill him here, it will be a big international mess," one of them said, his tone was polished but fearful.

.   .   .

"We are here for a job and we'll do it one way or the other. I have already sent one of our men outside disguised in Carlos's jacket. The CCTVs have recorded the footage, so for the world Carlos left the embassy forty minutes after he arrived. About that bitch, omit any record that she was here today. She called in sick today and you have no idea where she is, this will be the story. Got it?" To Jessica it felt as if the Ambassador was still not convinced, because when the second man spoke again his tone was threatening. "I don't know how you will do it, but shut the fuck up. Joaquin is not the one to tolerate dissent during a job, and I'm sure you would like to live."

The door opened again and closed. Jessica waited for a few minutes before putting in the tiny cam to check the lobby. It was deserted.

She considered going out and checking the Ambassador's office. After contemplating the pros and cons, she decided to go for it. With the SIG in her right hand, she stealthily made her way out to the lobby and placed herself silently outside the Ambassador's office. There was no sound, maybe they had left. She carefully slipped the tiny lens under the wooden door, checking the screen as the cam moved left and right. The room was empty, and she couldn't ascertain any booby traps. She wanted to go inside but then retreated to the PA's room and switched on her mic to apprise others of the development.

On the second floor, Wick had already finished scanning each room when he heard Jessica.

.   .   .

"If they sent a man outside, that means we have fifteen men to deal with. Three are dead, so that leaves us with twelve hostiles plus the Ambassador," Wick said.

"Yes," Jessica replied.

"Stan, what's your position?"

"I'm holed up in a room in the south wing on my floor with no visibility of outside."

"Jessica, do one thing. Find the CCTV room on the first floor. Get Mac's help to power the cams. Mac, once the cams are on, here's what I want you to do next." Wick took less than a minute to explain his improvised plan to the three of them, who couldn't help but smile.

# CHAPTER 28

"WHERE THE HELL IS MATIAS?" Joaquin snapped to no one in particular. "He should have been back by now. If he cannot take care of a stupid woman, what is he good for?"

They were in Carpio's suite on the fourth floor. Carlos was with them, tied to a chair his face was bruised and his left eye was swollen.

"Take a count of the men and ask Matias to report," Joaquin ordered Felipe. "And what's the status of the acid?"

"Johan spoke with the driver. He is twenty minutes away," Felipe said.

"He has one thing to do and he still managed to fuck it up." Johan wasn't in the room and Felipe didn't want to defend him.

He also didn't want himself to be a target of Joaquin's ire, so he quietly asked his men to check in. All ten, except Matias and his two men, checked in.

"Nicolás, find Matias. He was on the second floor. Take your men with you," Felipe barked the order on the sat phone to the man on the third floor.

⊏⊐

Wick was hiding in the third office from the North Wing's restroom on the second floor, belonging to someone named Mario Palazzo – the multilateral secretariat of the consulate, when he heard the fire exit door open and shut. His immediate reaction was to point his weapon at the door.

They must be here for the three men who lay dead in the bath-room. It was the only possibility.

Three distinct footsteps, checking every room, and calling the names of their colleagues. The footsteps slowly crept towards the room Wick was in. He waited, his Beretta ready. The foot-steps got louder, and Wick's posture tensed, bracing for the door to be flung open, followed by a reckless barrage of bullets.

Someone stopped right outside his room. Wick saw the door-knob rotate. The gate opened, but then he heard a loud shout. Someone was calling the man standing outside his room. Maybe they had found the bodies because the door never opened fully and was left hanging midway. The man's footsteps receded quickly down the corridor. If they had discovered the bodies, the next thing would be to inform Joaquin. Three dead men would cause a whole lot more damage than if they would have been alive. He couldn't let it happen. He gently walked towards the opened door and peeked in the direction of the footsteps.

One man was at the north wing's bathroom door, two others were advancing towards it. Wick saw their postures changing as they peered inside. The one with cropped hair moved to take out his sat phone.

From his protruding position, Wick instinctively leveled his Beretta and fired a round in the back of his skull. The sat phone fell to the floor. The man was dead before he even hit the floor. There was no blood, no spilled guts, no graphic explosion of gore. Just a well-placed shot crumpling the man, killing him instantly.

The other two took a moment longer to react. Wick had already measured them. The one, nearest to the dead man and farthest from Wick seemed to be the dominant one in the pack. His erect stance, straight shoulders and confident body language made him the next target. He was already in motion, turning in Wick's direction, simultaneously raising his weapon when the lead outdid him by a millisecond. But this gave the third assaulter time to find his aim. He shot at Wick while diving to his left, trying to find a vantage point. The bullet battered the door frame, a millimeter from where Wick's head was. Splinters soared in the air. Wick threw the door wide open and dived outside the room.

The move took the assaulter by surprise. He had expected Wick to duck inside and not dive outside. Wick lay sideways on the floor. His Beretta found its aim and coughed once. The advantage of those few milliseconds Wick gained due to the confusion in his opponent's mind gave him enough time to pierce his right eye, finishing him off instantly. Three more dead.

The Glocks and his Beretta had powerful silencers, but Wick wasn't sure if they had muffled the sounds enough. He paused and listened closely for any signs of movement in the hall above.

Then, he heard someone coming through the fire exit.

# CHAPTER 29

JESSICA WAS in the CCTV room when she heard the report of weapons. Gunfight on the floor above.

"Wick, can you hear me?" She spoke into the microphone, worried that the shots she'd heard had been directed towards him. No response. Perhaps his mic was off.

"Mac, I have done what you have asked me, now what?"

"Now, we have to wait for the reboot process to finish."

"Wick's comms is off. I'm going to check the second floor."

"Okay," Mac responded.

.  .  .

She slipped out of the room and then to the fire escape stairs. Her SIG sweeping from left to right, its suppressed barrel looking for possible targets. She paused at the fire exit door of the second floor waiting to hear something. She then opened it very slowly.  The hallway was vacant. She moved on the carpet with soft steps, her eyes darting from one side to the other.

"Stan, can you hear me?"

"Yes. Were those gunshots?"

"Yes. I'm looking into it." There was only one way to know - search every room on the floor. She pushed the first door to her right, and it swung open. Inside, she found a center table with open peanut packets strewn on it and three chairs. In a corner, there were two duffel bags. She checked the bathroom next, it was empty. The duffel bags had ID cards and some spare clothes. She also found a day old edition of El Universal—a well-known Venezuela daily.

"Jessica!" Wick's voice traveled over the static.

"Second floor, first room to the right from the south fire escape stairs."

"Okay. Wait there, I am coming over."

· · ·

Seconds later the door opened, and Wick appeared at the door.

"What happened? I heard gunshots," Jessica said

"Had to take down three hostiles."

# CHAPTER 30

STAN HAD HEARD the distinct sound of shots being fired on the floor below his. And if he had heard them, so would have others. Sprinting footsteps in the lobby confirmed his suspicions and his heart raced. He didn't know if they were coming for him or to the second floor.

"You and you! Check each room," someone yelled in the third floor's lobby.

Doors were being opened and shut in the lobby. There was no way Stan could face multiple hostiles alone in a confined space. He grabbed his SIG Sauer P320 from his waistband and threw it into the dustbin under the desk. He then grabbed the floor scrub brush and a tile cleaner solution from his cleaning bucket and went into the bathroom. It was a farfetched plan, but it was the best he could think of. He undid his ponytail, hiding his earpiece behind his long hair. Getting on his knees, he started rubbing the bathroom floor, but his ears remained glued to the main door. Seconds later, there was someone at the bathroom's entrance.

"Who are you? What are you doing here?"

"Good morning, sir." Stan turned his head and looked at the man, feigning surprise. He had a perfect getup. No one would have doubted him for a second in regular circumstances, but these were not normal circumstances.

"What are you doing here?"

"Cleaning... tiles...." Stan stuttered in broken English.

"Everyone has left for the day. " the man growled.

Stan gave him a bewildered look. "But the supervisor told me nothing. My walkie is also not working."

"How long have you been in this room?"

"This is my fourth room, sir," Stan lied.

"Did you hear anything?"

.   .   .

"What?"

"Nothing. Your work is over. Get up and get out."

"But... sir..."

"But what?"

"Nothing." He put the cleaner and the brush back in his bucket.
"Wash hands?" He raised his hands, palms out.

The man nodded.

Stan turned on the faucet and put his hands under the running
water. He glanced in the mirror and saw the man talking to
someone on his phone while watching Stan.

"Good night, sir." He wiped his hands at the back of his pants.
The man was still on the phone. Stan crossed him and left the
room. The lobby was deserted, but multiple rooms were open.

He turned to his left towards the nearest stairs to the second
floor.

.   .   .

"He is from the cleaning crew," Stan heard the man saying it to someone on the other side of his conversation. He had found a window of opportunity and he had to use it. He started to walk briskly towards the stairs when he heard someone stepping in the lobby behind him.

"Hey." Someone yelled and Stan had to stop. One more person stepped in the lobby behind the first man, trying to hide his gun holster. Stan instinctively caught his motion, but realized at once that he shouldn't have done that. The motion was instinctive but not so overt that a civilian would have paid any heed to it. Stan wasn't a civilian. He knew what he was looking for. The first one caught Stan's gaze but said nothing. It was a micro-expression that could be misconstrued easily. "Who are you?" he asked instead.

"I am…" Stan started to relay his scripted line when the man who'd found him came out of the room.

"Change of plans. You are coming with us?"

"Where… sir?" Stan stuttered.

"Johan, search him." He ordered one of the two men. The man named Johan stepped forward. Stan knew he would find nothing. The SIG was already disposed of.

. . .

Johan carefully patted  him down. "He's clean."

Stan remained silent all along cooperating with them. His every move was under scrutiny.

"Stan?" His earpiece suddenly mumbled, and he instinctively jerked his right hand upwards but the man standing next to him caught his wrist midway. Guns were now pointing at his forehead.

"Johan, check if there is anything in that room." Johan followed orders. Then without warning, the man hit Stan's left knee pit and he stumbled onto the floor.

"This is a nice gun." Johan was smiling at the door. He had Stan's discarded SIG Sauer P320 in his hand.

"Forgetting something?" The man who had just hit him, pointed his gun's barrel at Stan's head giving a cold grin.

Wick and Jessica heard Stan's cries on their earpieces and knew they had to do act fast.

# CHAPTER 31

"WHAT HAPPENED?" Mac too sensed something was wrong.

"We don't know for sure. Worst case, they have taken Stan. Whatever it is, we have no time before they come for us. Change the frequencies of the channel. If they get hold Stan's device, we'll still be able to talk to each other," Wick said.

"Okay."

"Where are we on the CCTV?"

"Jessica has restarted it, but the system is bloody ancient - taking ages to reboot. Will need some more time."

. . .

"Okay, once the cams are online, find out where they have taken Sam," Wick said.

"On it."

"Talk to you soon."

# CHAPTER 32

"WE HAVE AN INFILTRATOR."

Felipe brought his phone to his ear. "Say again."

"We have an infiltrator on the third floor."

"Who?"

"He pretended to be from the cleaning crew, but we've found an earpiece and a gun from him."

Felipe looked at Joaquin, who signaled to bring Stan to the room. Felipe relayed the message.

. . .

No one knew about this operation except Joaquin's men and Henrique. Even Carpio had only been given information on a need-to-know basis, so the leak couldn't have come from him. He stared at Carlos who looked defeated. It couldn't be him either. Then how had this man gotten in?

The door opened and three of his men brought in a man in cleaning crew uniform. His left eye was swollen and there was a fresh cut on the right side of his lip. The man seemed beaten, yet there was hope in his eyes. Joaquin couldn't fathom why.

Carlos let out an audible gasp. Stan observed him from the corner of his eye. His face was an image of defeat. He had accepted his own death hours ago, perhaps the moment he met Joaquin. He was staring into the distance. Terrified. Shaking.

Stan slyly observed the rest of the room. Six people in total, including the Ambassador. All carrying Glocks except Carpio. Two twelve-gauge pump action shotguns lay on the bed. The man with the scar stood tall among them. Joaquin Thomas.

"Who are you?" Joaquin demanded.

"I am from the cleaning crew," Stan spoke with a fake Austrian accent. The longer he could continue with his act, the more time he could gain for Wick and Jessica.

.   .   .

"From when did the cleaning crew come to work with a gun and a listening device?" Joaquin laughed hard and then bent to grab Stan's throat. "Listen, shithead, if I have to ask this question one more time, I'll pump so much lead into your skull that your bosses will not even recognize you. You understand me?" He brought his face close to Stan's and uttered each syllable, "Do you understand me?"

The man wasn't bluffing, Stan knew that. He contemplated his position. He had to decide and had to decide quickly. Joaquin's stare turned murkier. He could see that Stan was thinking of something. He raised Stan's SIG and before Stan could even react, squeezed the trigger. The 9mm lead tore into his thigh muscle and Stan screamed his guts out.

"Who. Are. You?" Joaquin asked again.

"I..." Stan's breathing was heavy.

He tried to keep a brave face, but it was tough. Especially when, for the first time in his life, he was certain he was going to die.

BAM. BAM. The second floor was rocked by two gunshots.

# CHAPTER 33

JOAQUIN GAVE his men a confused look but then his expression transformed into rage. "Damn you?" he yelled at Stan before shooting him twice on his leg. Stan screamed hard. Joaquin then swung a kick. With no strength to block the move, Stan lay in his crosshairs; only closing his eyes seconds before the boot crashed into his chest. An explosion of violent pain rose in his body and his cries reverberated in the room. The force sent him skidding a few feet across the floor. Blood loss and the pain had squeezed every grain of his strength. His mind faded into darkness. Dazed. Disoriented.

"I told you. I bloody told you." Carpio was in panic.

Joaquin ignored him. He was rubbing his head with both hands, panting hard, thinking through this mess. His last job was turning out to be a damn disaster. "Find them. Whoever they are, I want all of them dead," He roared at Felipe who swung into action.

———

Gunshots in the consulate had not only brought an urgency on the fourth floor, but they also woke up the sleepy main street. The passersby started to retreat to safety. Someone dialed the police emergency number.

———

Away from all this chaos, on the second floor, Jessica and Wick were hard at work. They had brought the ammo bag from the janitor room on the first floor. Wick positioned himself at the south flank while Jessica manned the opposite wing. Elevators, the main stairs, and the fire escape - all within their view.

Jessica heard it first. Multiple footsteps rumbled in the fire exit stairs. Another set of footsteps were coming down heavily on the main stairs, closer to the south flank - Wick's location.

"Now!" Jessica hissed in her earpiece and three smoke grenades hit the floor in unison.

———

Inside the minivan, Mac and Jakob stared at each other. Their hearts, pumping blood at thrice the normal speed. The air was charged by police sirens rushing to the consulate.

"We should move from here," Jakob suggested.

.  .  .

"I cannot risk the connection being broken now. Go outside. Open the hood. Look busy," Mac said.

Jakob considered it for a second longer but then got out.

━━━━

Felipe stopped at the edge of the main stairs. The hallway was drowned in darkness and smoke.

"Johan, you in position?" He spoke on the sat phone to the other team waiting at the fire exit stairs. The fire exit was at a bend so the teams could not see each other either.

"Yes." Johan looked at his two teammates. From the sliver of the fire exit door, they could see that the lobby was dark, deserted and hazy.

"How's the visibility at your side?" Felipe asked.

"Not good."

"Can you see any movement?" Felipe asked.

"No."

.  .  .

A second later, both teams heard someone running away from the main stairs and towards the fire exit. A shadow was moving.

Felipe and his men leveled their SMGs and started to spray bullets at the shadow from behind. Johan and his men saw the shadow approaching them. Their guns blazed at the silhouette but the target opened a door and vanished inside, shutting it with a bang.

"He is boxed in a room. We are closing in. Back us up," Johan whispered in his sat phone. He and his men took positions outside the room. Felipe and his team sprinted towards the room.

Inside the room, Jessica checked the street outside the window. Unlike the main street, the side alley was still deserted. A few parked cars on the side but no one was lurking. It would not remain so for long. She could hear the police loudspeakers. They must be cordoning off the main street. This alley was, possibly, next in line. She tucked her gun in the holster, slid the window pane open and climbed out onto the ledge, balancing herself against the wall. She slowly made her way to the adjacent room's window, in the direction of the fire exit. The window pane of that room was already up. She climbed inside and took her position, waiting for Wick's signal.

Felipe signaled to Johan to enter the room with his men; he and the man accompanying him decided to wait outside. Johan nodded and rotated the knob anticlockwise; throwing the door wide open. Inside, there was a foyer opening into a larger space. The room was dark but the visibility was better than the hallway. Johan entered first, knees slightly bent. Two of his colleagues followed him. With his left hand, he flicked the light switch. The room was vacant.

On the opposite side of the lobby a door opened, and Wick stepped out. In his right hand, he held an Uzi. He could see two shadows closer to his side of the wall. He brought the Uzi to chest height and pulled the trigger.

The bullets raced at seven hundred meters per minute to penetrate their targets. The barrel suppressed the report, but it was only effective in noisy areas, not in the eerie quiet of the consulate. The SMG had been noisy, but he didn't care anymore. Johan and his men inside the room heard the noise and ducked instinctively. The sound came from the lobby. Johan turned, lying on the floor, in time to see Felipe falling to the ground.

The shots stopped as soon as Wick knew the job was done. Felipe's sat phone crackled. Johan knew who it would be, but he didn't dare go out of the room to pick it up.

The next call was on his sat phone. "What happened?" Joaquin's voice betrayed no worry.

"Felipe is dead."

.  .  .

"Two down." Jessica heard Wick over the earpiece. "Lobby clear," Wick confirmed. His Uzi was still pointed at the door. There wasn't any movement outside. She knew that the men in the room wouldn't dare venture out, knowing someone would be aiming for their heads. As soon as she received Wick's confirmation, she opened her room's door and slid out towards the fire exit in a squat position. Once the handle was within Jessica's reach, she did two things in quick succession. One, she tossed two grenades into the open room where Johan and his men were holed up. Two, she opened the fire escape door and got out, shutting it hard behind her.

Johan was thinking of his next steps when he saw the first grenade rolling into the room. His men saw it too.

As soon as the door touched the frame, the grenade blew up.

Johan wasted no time in getting up. His men followed suit, leaping out the window. Still, the twin explosion caught them in mid-air and the three bodies crashed on the street. Their backs burned, but the falling debris from the blast gave them no chance.

▭

Behind the police line, TV crews had gathered at the edge of the police line when the Uzi stopped roaring. Every lens zoomed to the second floor. The grenade blasts came two minutes later with three bodies flying out of the second floor. Five officers ran towards the side alley to assess the damage.

.   .   .

"Medics! NOW!" one of them shouted to the ambulance parked near the building. The attendants grabbed their supplies and sprinted to the location. Lenses followed them. Police quickly cordoned off the alley to stop them. Police radios were chattering incessantly taking stock of the situation. Guns were blazing and bombs were going off on the most peaceful street of Vienna, and no one knew why.

# CHAPTER 34

DESPITE BEING SOUNDPROOFED, the fourth-floor suite felt the reverberations from the twin blasts. The sat- phone in Joaquin's hand went blank. Joaquin grasped that he had just lost his men to the unidentified assailants. He saw fear on the faces of his men in the room; none relished the prospect of fighting an enemy they knew nothing about.

"What now?" Carpio spoke in a quivering voice. He was standing near the bed, shaking badly. This was nothing like he'd planned for. "The police are outside. The consulate is ruined, and you still have no clue who you're dealing with."

"Shut up, you bloody idiot." Joaquin chewed his lips.

"How dare you? I thought you were a mastermind but…" Carpio was yelling and at the same time shuddering with fear and anger. "Everything is a mess. Your men are dead, and you cannot wrap your head around the situation." With every word he spewed, he was regaining his confidence. In his anger he grabbed the shotgun lying on the bed, waving it dangerously at Joaquin. "You killed Ana, you will kill Carlos and this man too, but this will not stop. The president will throw you to the dogs. You are d..." A bullet hissed through the air and before Carpio could finish his sentence, he was dead. His body pushed back in the air and landed on the middle of the bed, the shotgun flew away from his lifeless hand and landed behind the bed's steel headboard.

"Anyone else has anything to add?" Joaquin asked around the room. None of his men responded. He glanced at Carlos who was shuddering with fear while Stan was still unconscious. "It's all because of you. Should've killed you the moment I saw you." Joaquin yelled at Carlos.

Axel, any ideas?" Joaquin was getting desperate. Axel nodded his head.

"Gael? Jorge?" They shook their heads too.

"Shit. Shit. Shit," Joaquin yelled helplessly.

The three men had never seen Joaquin cornered like this. They all agreed that he had anger issues, but he was never short of ideas. Till today. Today, he had killed the one man he should not have killed—Carpio and had kept one man alive whom he shouldn't have - Carlos. If nothing else - Carpio would have been the key to get them out of here unscathed. Not anymore.

"Joaquin." a voice burst out from the sat phone in Joaquin's palm. He jerked, staring at the receiver in surprise. The three men and Carlos too were taken aback.

"I didn't want to kill you or your men, but I had to," the voice continued. "You can still live. Give me Carlos and the other guy and I will leave."

"Who do you think you are talking to?"

"I know who I am talking to. You want Carlos dead. I want him to breathe, but now we both have a problem. Police are outside; the building is surrounded. There is no way for any of us to get out of here alive unless we help each other." Wick spoke into Felipe's sat phone.

"I'm not scared of death and I don't give a damn what you say. Carlos has to die and along with him your friend will too."

"You can kill Carlos a week later or a month later but not today. Today is not your day. Talk to your men. Ask them what they want. I'll call you in five minutes." Wick disconnected the call.

. . .

"What's your plan?" Jessica looked at Wick.

"I am going in. I want to meet this man before killing him."

"You sure?" Jessica looked worried.

"Go to the ambassador's office and do what we discussed. I will be there soon."

"Okay." Jessica took the main stairs.

Wick then hissed into his earpiece. "Mac when I say NOW, cut the electricity to the fourth floor."

"Done."

Wick reconnected Joaquin's line. "You asked your men?"

"Why should I trust you?"

"You have a better option?" Wick responded to his question with a question.

.   .   .

"You killed eleven of my men."

"If I hadn't, they would have killed me."

"I still don't see a reason to trust you."

"One way or the other, the Police will be in the building soon. You and I both do not have enough firepower to fight with a battalion. Our survival depends on teaming up."

"Why Carlos?"

"I took a contract to keep him safe. I don't give a fuck if you kill him tomorrow. Once I'm out of here, he is not my problem. He is the passport to my payment. Dead Carlos is of no use to me."

"I can kill him and your friend right now."

"I think you shouldn't because then I will kill you and your men," Wick said it in a matter of fact tone.

"How dare you threaten me?" Joaquin yelled. His men glanced nervously at each other. The man on the other side was either a psycho or out of his mind.

. . .

"I've killed eleven men today and I am still in one piece talking to you. So, if it comes to that, don't harbor any illusion that I won't do it."

Wick's tone made Joaquin pause. The man on the other side was his enemy, but he was also right. Joaquin himself was a remorseless killer, and he could feel in his gut that his opponent wasn't bluffing. The scary thing was that the man spoke all this in an unusually calm tone. Even after killing so many of Joaquin's men, he could still think straight. At least straighter than Joaquin himself. There was no harm in hearing him out, if for nothing other than to take stock of the man. And within this room, Joaquin had the advantage of numbers.

"Who else is with you?" Joaquin responded, calmer this time.

"No one."

"Come to the fourth floor. Unarmed. One of my men will meet you outside and bring you in. If you try anything funny, I will shoot you and everyone else you care about in this building."

Wick thought for a moment. "Okay." And then disconnected the call.

# CHAPTER 35

AXEL PATTED Wick down and took his Beretta before bringing him into the suite. Joaquin stood ten feet away from the door. His men - Gael was to Wick's left, Jorge stood diagonally behind Joaquin, and Axel took position behind Wick, manning the suite's entrance. Axel pushed Wick from behind and he stumbled forward, stopping closer to Joaquin than he would have wanted. But once he steadied, he quickly took stock of the room. It was almost two thousand square feet. A large king size metallic bed rested at the center. Carpio's dead body was on the bed, coloring the sheets red. The suite's large windows were covered with thick dark drapes. The walls looked thicker than usual. Wick expected a couple of rows of stud placements, one along each interior side, to soundproof the room, a perfect setting for murder without letting the world know about it.

In a corner, Carlos was tied to a chair, staring at him. His face was a mess, his clothes bloodied. Stan was on the floor in the opposite corner, bleeding, but breathing. He wasn't moving, though, which was a bad sign, but Wick decided to worry about him later.

"Ah!" Joaquin exclaimed, looking Wick up and down. "Good to meet the man who killed so many of mine." He was back in his element now that his enemy was unarmed.

Joaquin waited for Wick to respond while checking him up close. The man who'd decimated his entire plan and killed his eleven men single-handedly.

Wick said nothing, instead keeping his focus on Joaquin. He wanted to gauge his adversary before going further. Knowing his background, Wick understood why he was the one leading this group of mercenaries. Hovering somewhere around six foot, Joaquin was strong, with a muscle-packed tall frame. His bald head shone under the fluorescent lamp. A Glock in his left hand. Just from the expressions in his eyes, Wick knew he would have no qualms killing all three of them—Carlos, Stan, and Wick— without a second thought. But he wouldn't, at least for the time being.

"American?" Joaquin asked.

Wick gestured at Carlos and Stan, sidestepping the question. "These are mine."

. . .

Joaquin's expressions hardened. 'I don't think so. You should have stayed out of my business.' He growled and moved dangerously towards Wick.

"NOW," Wick barked taking a step back.

Mac pressed the keypad, and the timer started.

*Three.*

Moving forward, Joaquin swung his right-punch at Wick's face. Wick blocked it with both hands, but the massive force made him wobble. **Joaquin's raised left hand aimed** Glock at Wick's head.

*Two.*

For Wick, everything happened in slow motion.

*One.*

The room drowned in the darkness. Wick closed his eyes and rubbed his eyelids to get accustomed to the darkness. When he opened his eyes, he was ready for the dark; his opponents weren't.

·  ·  ·

The sudden dimness surprised Joaquin, but he had already squeezed the trigger. There was a moment's difference between the descending darkness and the muzzle flash. As soon as the light went off, Wick had dived to the floor. Everyone in the room heard a man scream. The bullets had found a target. Axel's lifeless body bashed the door with a thump. The pungent smell of gunpowder filled the room.

*One man down. Three left.*

Wick, in a well-rehearsed move, focused on Joaquin's knee cap. He had already perceived the distance when monitoring Joaquin. He swung his boot at Joaquin's right knee cap hitting it sideways. He knew that the kick wasn't powerful enough, but Joaquin's cries indicated that the impact was enough. Wick saw the silhouette crumple to the ground grabbing its knee. He also heard the Glock hitting the floor away from both of them. It was time to take on the other two.

He changed his stance, moving towards Gael, who was to his left. Wick's eyes were accustomed to the darkness, Gael's weren't. Wick saw his outline as he tried to find Wick while standing in the same place.

Wick reached closer, grabbed his flailing wrist, and with a swift movement twisted it at an odd angle. With a snapping sound, it became useless. Gael stumbled backward with a cry, grabbing the broken wrist with his other hand.

.   .   .

Wick crouched and took out his K-BAR military blade from his leg strap sheath and thrust it into Gael's neck twice... before releasing the blade.

*Two down. Two left.*

Wick moved to Jorge - his next target. Jorge saw something approaching him. His body tensed. He turned to face his assailant, but Wick had already swung a knuckle punch aiming at his nose. Jorge spat blood with a loud cry, covering his nose with both hands, leaving his gun. Wick's boot collided with Jorge's chest and he hit the wall behind him, falling on the ground. Wick took no time to arch his back, wrap his legs around Jorge's neck, tense them until a cracking sound confirmed that his neck was broken.

*Three down. Joaquin left.*

Joaquin could hear the cries while stumbling in the dark with one useless knee. He was at a loss; far removed from his element. This wasn't anticipated. He wasn't ready for this. His only option was to find his gun. He furiously swept the floor with both hands and eventually found the butt of the Glock. Trying to get back on his feet, he turned in the direction of the last sound he heard and saw a man. Without thinking he opened fire.

Wick saw Joaquin getting on his feet with the gun and he ducked behind the bed's headboard. The muzzle flash lit the dark room. The bullets cut a rough line into the headboard from left to right. Expletives followed the shots fired. The bullets grazed the wall plaster just above his head. Wick was already sweeping the floor for anything to counter Joaquin. His efforts bore fruit soon when his left knee touched the barrel of the same shotgun that Carpio had been waving madly. He used his left hand to pull it towards him. The weight of the gun meant that it was loaded. He waited for Joaquin to waste his magazine which didn't take long. Joaquin heard his gun coughing without bullets and paused to load another magazine. It was Wick's turn.

**BOOM!**

Joaquin's left leg gave way under him, and he fell to the ground, screaming.

**BOOM!**

This time it was the chest. The buckshot exited through his back, taking his life with it.

Three minutes later, the backup supply kicked in and the power was restored. The fluorescent lights illuminated the room again.

**BOOM!**

.   .   .

In the light, Wick fired one last time at Jorge, who was still squirming, and his body jerked lifelessly on the carpet. He looked at Carlos who was staring back at him with fear.

Amidst the massacre Wick stood calm, to an almost unsettling degree.

# CHAPTER 36

THE ELEVATOR OPENED in Carpio's office on the first floor. Jessica, who was already in the office, had her SIG out, pointing at the ground but ready for anything.

The elevator doors opened, and Carlos came out first, limping, weak but relieved. Wick came next, carrying Stan on his right shoulder. His wounds were tied with a dry cloth.

"Everything's ready?" Wick asked.

"Yes," Jessica replied. She ambled forward and lent Stan her shoulder to lean on.

"You both go on. I need to take care of something else," Wick said.

.  .  .

"Okay," Jessica said.

"Carlos, I need you to come with me." Wick turned to Carlos, signaling towards the door and they both exited the room.

"Mac, I will send you the location. Be ready." Jessica spoke into her earpiece once Carlos left with Sam.

"Okay." Mac was ecstatic.

Wick and Carlos took the main stairs to the second floor. Carlos was walking slightly ahead of Wick and as soon as he stepped in the lobby, he took a step back. The smoke had subsided and all he could see was destruction and dead bodies. It was a carnage he had only heard about but never witnessed, not even as a human activist.

Wick could understand the shock, but he had no time to spare. Things were moving fast, and he still had to finish the last leg of the mission.

"We need to hurry." Wick patted him on his shoulder.

"Yeah... yeah... sure," Carlos stammered moving forward. "But where are we going?"

.  .  .

"To that restroom." Wick pointed to the door at the end of the lobby. "Open it."

Carlos walked to the door and did what was told. The bathroom floor was slick with blood. Three more dead bodies. None of them shot. Carlos covered his mouth in horror.

"Can you open that?" Wick pointed at the closet's door. Carlos gazed at Wick and then stepped inside gingerly, avoiding the blood. Inside the closet, Ana jerked back in fright.

"Ana?" Carlos was surprised to see her alive.

"Carlos." She got up and hugged him, crying.

"I thought you were dead."

"I almost died. A man saved me and asked me to wait here."

"Him?" Carlos stepped aside and Ana looked towards the door. No one was there.

"Hello, you there?" Carlos yelled.

.    .    .

No response. Carlos looked back at Ana, helping her to come out of the restroom. Outside, the lobby was deserted.

"He was just here," He said.

"Who?" Ana asked.

"The man who saved me. I didn't even get a chance to thank him."

"Me too." She knew whom Carlos was talking about. "Who else is alive?" she asked.

"No one."

"Carpio?"

"Dead."

"Jesus!" Ana covered her mouth with her hand.

"What should we do?"

.  .  .

"Call the police," Ana suggested. She was now in control.

"They are already outside."

"Then I need to make some calls. Wait here," Ana said and opened the nearest office in the lobby to find a phone.

# CHAPTER 37

MAC AND JAKOB reached the location sent by Jessica, five blocks away from the consulate building. Stan and Jessica were waiting for them. A three-foot square shaped steel cover was swung open behind them.

"Where's Wick?"

"He's coming."

"You okay?" Mac looked at Stan's wound.

"Hmm," Stan said, groggily.

Fifteen minutes later, Wick appeared at the opening.

. . .

"What were you doing?" Jessica asked, helping him slide the steel cover back to its original position.

"Tying some loose ends," he said cryptically, getting into the van.

Jakob took over the wheels and the van lurched forward.

"What about Carlos?"

"He's safe."

"How did you find this passage?" Jakob was curious.

Mac looked at Wick, who seemed unwilling to talk. Jessica nudged Mac to go ahead. "During my analysis of the consulate's blueprints, I identified a glitch. The wall behind the Ambassador's chair had three times the thickness required. On further research, I found that the building layouts were changed two years ago. At around the same time Carpio took charge. In the original blueprint, the wall was of the right width. So what changed? After landing in Vienna, when Jessica and Stan had gone out with you, Sam and I worked on this. As per Sam's estimate, there should have been something in that fake wall." Mac paused, letting Jessica carry it forward.

. . .

"When Wick sent me to switch on the CCTV cams, he asked me to check the office first. I found a hidden door, the same shade as the wall, so not visible to the naked eye. But it had the same security system as that of that private elevator in his office. It needed Carpio's ID card to open it. He must had this built as an escape route. When Sam killed Joaquin, he picked up the ambassador's ID card and handed it to me," Jessica said.

"But why would he need a secret tunnel?" Jakob asked.

"Maybe he suspected that one day the President or his minions might come for him and he needed to have a plan ready?" Jessica replied.

"Maybe but how did you know where the room opened?" Jakob asked.

"We didn't. It was a risk that we took. The fact that it was a secret route meant that the purpose was to get away from the consulate and it must open in a secluded place or alley far away from the building," Mac completed the story.

"And that's why we had to wait for them to send us their location." Jakob chuckled.

"Absolutely." Mac smiled.

# CHAPTER 38

HENRIQUE WAS STARING at the television screen. The Venezuelan consulate building in Vienna was rocked with blasts and gunshots. Sixteen people were dead, including the Ambassador. It was a catastrophe of unimaginable magnitude.

His face color paled when Carlos appeared on the screen, ready to give any and every detail to the media. How the President and Henrique wanted him dead and had sent his men to kill him on Austrian soil.

Henrique could see the writing on the wall. The story would run for months on prime time, and Carlos would be at the center of it as a survivor of an inhuman regime. People would look for a scapegoat and Henrique knew who it would be.

"Sir, the President wants to talk to you." His secretary was at the door.

. . .

"Tell him I am on my way to meet him."

His secretary took the message and closed the door behind her.

He grabbed his coat and car keys. He knew what he had to do. There was no way he would get mercy for this. Everyone in his family would also be prosecuted and killed in broad daylight. It was better to die on his own than to be tortured to death. He thought of his eight-year-old son, and his eyes turned moist.

# CHAPTER 39

**FIVE DAYS LATER**

"A ten minute long video has surfaced online today," the news anchor announced enthusiastically. "It's a recorded version of what happened in the deceased Venezuelan ambassador's office in Vienna when the New York Times columnist Mr. Carlos arrived there. The video shows how the Ambassador and Venezuelan mercenaries planned the whole thing. Ms. Ana, the Minister-Counselor, who has since taken refuge in Austria, was also shown being assaulted. The uploader has mentioned that he has more such videos and would not hesitate to release them if the Venezuelan President does not resign within the next two days on account of the reprehensible human rights violations in his country, of which this incident is the most recent. The international community is already putting massive pressure on the incumbent Venezuela President to resign and face an inquiry. Although the President has denied his involvement in this debacle, no one is convinced, not even Russia, one of his staunch allies. We will keep updating you as we get more details on this international scandal." The newscaster excused herself for an commercial break.

---

The doorbell rang and Karina answered the door. It was a guy from the postal department.

"Please sign here," he requested, handing her an envelope.

"Who is it?" Carlos yelled from inside.

"Post." She took the heavy envelope.

Carlos walked into the hall, bandaged, and still limping. Karina was already closing the door.

"Who sent it?" he asked.

"No name." She handed the envelope to him.

He tore the envelope and took out the documents. There was a small note along with them.

Best wishes for a happy married life.

.   .   .

They quickly checked the rest of the papers. They were signed. Everything was in order. Carlos looked at Karina, she was already crying. He smiled and wrapped her in a tight embrace. Their hearts were thankful to their God and to the one woman who had just delivered them the best gift of their lives.

# CHAPTER 40

ANA WAS in the shower when her cell phone rang. She picked up her bathrobe and came out of the bathroom, but by then the phone had stopped ringing. She checked the number; it was a private one.

She looked at the door. It was locked. The window panes were covered with heavy drapes. She was on the tenth floor, all alone in the apartment and was expecting this call.

The phone rang again after a gap of ninety-one seconds. Ana picked up the call after four rings.

"How are you?" the modulated voice asked.

"I am good. Thanks for the apartment."

. . .

"We take care of our own."

"I can see that."

"Heard you faced some problems in the consulate with Joaquin's men."

"Nothing worth mentioning."

"Whatever happened to you still needs to come out in public. Sympathy is a powerful tool in the hands of the right people."

"I understand."

"We have also received information that your President had signed an order to appoint you as the next Venezuelan Ambassador to the US. You will soon get the official word."

Ana said nothing but she was ecstatic. Professor knew about her ambitions to attain that position and he had delivered it rather too soon.

"You did well."

.   .   .

"Thank you, Professor. I only passed the information you gave me to McAvoy and his men in the TF-77 like you asked me to. McAvoy will never know that his asset in the consulate was playing him."

"We've delivered our side of the bargain, as promised." The man ignored that bit.

"I cannot thank you enough."

"It's time to deliver the rest of your side of the deal."

"I'm ready."

"You will get your chance soon. For now, we want you to enjoy." The voice paused. "Put this phone on speaker and remove the curtains."

Ana did as asked.

"Open the door and let the man standing outside come in."

Ana took a moment to register what Professor meant, but she dared not question him. She went and unlocked the main door. A muscular black man was waiting. He stepped inside without a word. She closed the door behind him and followed him to the bedroom.

"Drop your clothes," The voice ordered. Ana paused. This was getting weird and somewhat humiliating. The voice recognized her hesitation. "Is there a problem?"

"No, Professor," she said meekly and undid her bathrobe. She was wearing nothing underneath. The man in the room observed her with interest and then started to undress.

"Do what he tells you to." The voice said to Ana. "Adam, make sure it's a good show." This was for the man.

Ana was stunned, but Adam moved forward and grabbed her by the waist pulling her towards himself. She looked out the window and saw silhouettes on the tenth floor of the adjacent building, some hundred yards away, staring at her apartment.

It was a show, and she was starring in it.

# CHAPTER 41

MARYLAND, **USA**

Wick was staring at the image of an infant and his parents, taken on a bright summer day. The infant was staring back at him, but the faces of the parents were distorted beyond recognition. Wick knew it was done on purpose.

The old worn out photo had arrived via email in his personal mailbox. Apart from this one, there were two more unread emails for him. One of them offered him a lifetime free credit card while the other offered him a loan at low interest rates. Wick rarely used this mailbox. The photo had been sent to him four days ago, the same day he had landed in Maryland from Vienna. The same day he saved Carlos.

The sender's email was encrypted, and the subject line was, "Funny Picture- do not delete," which again was weird. The infant was Wick himself. He knew because he had seen his childhood photos in his school records. What about the other two people in the photo? Were they his parents? He suspected they might be. But what caught his attention was the one-line text in that email.

*"Want to find your parents? Find Professor."*

*THE END.*

## GET WICKED STORM
### Sam Wick universe book #2

**Do not forget to download your FREE COPY of The NSA Top Secret Report on SAM WICK.**
**Check www.thechaseaustin.com**

———

Thanks for reading this book. I hope you would have enjoyed it. Would you be interested in telling me your views on the story?

**LEAVE A REVIEW - USA**
**LEAVE A REVIEW - UK**
**LEAVE A REVIEW - AUSTRALIA**
**LEAVE A REVIEW - CANADA**
**LEAVE A REVIEW - INDIA**
**Goodreads Review**

Book reviews are not only important to you as a readers, but they are critically important to authors like me. As a novelist, I can tell you that I depend heavily on reviews from my readers.

They not only help others to find my books, but more importantly, they help me to improve my craft so the next book I write will be even better.

Well I am here to urge you, dear reader, to leave book reviews either on Amazon, Goodreads or BookBub.

## Where you can write review on the Amazon book page

Click the links above and they will open the respective review pages of my book in your preferred Amazon store.

Click the button "Write a customer review" (Please note that the words might vary in your country's amazon store)

On clicking the button, you will be taken to a page where you can rate the book from 1 to 5 stars (5 being the highest) and you can write a couple of line about the book.

If you face any issues, please let me know at *chaseaustincreative@gmail.com* and I will be glad to help you with the process.

# EXCERPT FROM WICKED KILL
## (SAM WICK BOOK #4)

**Sam Wick's new mission was simple - Infiltrate Iran, find the target and get out. Nothing could have gone wrong, except everything that could go wrong, went wrong.**

**Sam Wick's most explosive thriller, yet.**

Sam Wick is the one the Government calls on to extract people out of the worst of the worst enemy places on earth. Where the government cannot and will not go, he will. There is no guarantee that he'll succeed every time but he doesn't have a choice or does he?

For fans of Vince Flynn and Lee Child, a heart-pumping thriller of action, betrayal, split-second decisions and conspiracy by the Breakthrough Author Chase Austin.

What Readers are saying about Sam Wick's Adventures;

★★★★★ "One heck of an entertaining and intense ride... Fast, entertaining, suspenseful and action-packed... you will find yourself flying through and it will be hard to let it go!" - *Amazon Review*

★★★★★ *"Fast paced read with a Kick-Ass hero you can't help rooting for." - Amazon Review*

★★★★★ *"Full of awesome action. I can't wait to read the next book" - Amazon Review*

★★★★★ *" I did not put this book down for any reason other than to eat." - Amazon Review*

★★★★★ *"Fast paced, lots of thrills. Highly entertaining." - Amazon Review*

★★★★★ *"I'm ready for Sam's next assignment." - Amazon Review*

# CHAPTER 1

.

TEHRAN, **IRAN**

Dawn was just breaking, and sleepy street dogs were beginning to stir when Sam Wick completed his customary five-mile morning run. This was his third consecutive day in Tehran, the capital city of Iran, but he had been in the country in the past. He knew the place well, having spent a year or so here over the course of three previous missions. Apart from his usual run, he preferred to stay in the safe house the entire day, thinking, planning and honing the nuts and bolts of the plan. He needed the jog to take the edge off all the coffee he consumed during the day.

He checked his satellite phone—his communication line routed directly to the office of William Helms, Director of the NSA and Joint Custodian of Task Force-77, in Maryland, USA. The voice-secure sat phone was Wick's only direct link to Helms. No one else knew he was in Iran, and no one could. The administration would want complete deniability when the target was captured, even more so if anything went awry.

The safehouse was Task Force-77's property. Task Force-77, or TF-77, was a black ops team jointly overseen by the NSA and the US Army—an off-the-books team that came into play when diplomatic solutions failed. Powered with US military might across the globe and NSA's intel, the team was sent on the toughest missions in the most dangerous locations that required the use of means that no government could ever authorize officially. Its multiple assets were spread in sensitive locations across the globe, and Wick was one of the best assets TF-77 had ever produced. He was invariably chosen to undertake the riskiest exfiltration missions, especially in countries where the US could not intervene directly. Countries like Iran.

5'11". Weather-beaten face. Black hair. Pointed nose. Medium build. Unreadable sea-blue eyes and an unassuming walk. Trained in Krav Maga, Kalarippayattu and Muay Thai fighting styles. Expert in disguise. He'd been born in Kansas, but he could speak and write seventeen languages.

For anyone looking at him closely, he appeared a mass of contradictions. There was subsurface violence, almost always in control, but very much alive. There was also a pensiveness that seemed to stem from pain, yet he rarely gave vent to the anger that pain usually provoked.

.   .   .

Back in the safe house, he waited for the on-ground support team to arrive. To support field operatives during their missions the TF-77 deployed small on-the-ground teams—typically three to four members, depending on mission specifics. Although Wick had mentioned that he didn't need one for this mission, his bosses insisted that he take one as backup.

Wick had received a message on the TF-77 application on his cell phone. Olivia, Logan and Elijah—his support team—were on their way from Isfahan, a city in central Iran. Based on their travel plans, Wick expected them to reach the safe house in the next few hours.

This was Wick's first mission with this team. He had read their files, and they appeared competent. That's all he needed. Olivia would help him handle the logistics if required. The bonus was that she was an expert in a gunfight. Elijah was a former marine with tight credentials. Logan was a tech guy and a non-combatant. Wick had plans for each of them. If they were here, then he was fine to use them as he deemed fit in the overall mix. He had that authority. He knew that. They understood that.

He looked at his unique shopping list lying on the table. He knew where he would find the items. He had contacts in the city to get the things he needed. He grabbed his kurta to get ready. He had to get the items on his list and be back in the safe house before the support team arrived.

━━━

# CHAPTER 2

ON THAT SUNNY MORNING, the air was heavy. The azan echoed from the loudspeakers perched at the top of the watch-tower at the market square of one of the city's busiest markets.

Amid all this, Wick moved with purpose. An oversized long kurta, blue rugged jeans, black unkempt hair, and rectangular blue reading glasses gave him the look of a university student. He didn't need a false wig or eyebrows or beard to blend in with the locals. His blue eyes were the only thing that made him stand out in a place like this, and he was wearing brown contacts to hide them. Wick was aware that his physical characteristics were part of the reason that time and again he was chosen for such missions, but the more important factor was his ability to hit his targets fast and hard. Spending too long planning meant delays, and delays killed momentum. He hated that. His bosses hated that.

.   .   .

In the field, he had the final say. But he knew this power came with a lot of responsibility. One wrong decision could easily jeopardize America's image and future actions. His strategy was to minimize the factors of coincidence and luck in his missions, and the best way to do that was to do away with unnecessary antics. Keep things simple and uncomplicated. That was easier said than done in high-voltage missions like this which involved so many moving pieces. It had been a long road for him, with lots of ups and downs, to get to this stage where he now had the temperament to focus on just one thing and find the best way to get it without complications. His consistency had earned him the nickname 'the machine' from other TF-77 agents. Not that he knew or cared about such things. He was a loner and rarely spoke with anyone within the agency. There was no one in the world he could truly call his own. It was a tough way to live, but the only way he knew.

⊏▭⊐

Wick walked through the throngs, his eyes carefully soaking in every small detail of his vicinity. His walk was assured yet unpretentious.

He stopped at a nondescript phone booth shop with a signboard that quite unnecessarily announced: "Phone calls". In the age of cell phones, time seemed to have stood still for paid phone booths like this. People walked past, ignoring the run-down structure and its middle-aged owner. For them, neither existed in this modern world.

. . .

Wick was probably the only customer the shop owner had seen in days, maybe even months. Wick asked if he could make a call. The man looked at him and demanded, "You have the money?"

Wick produced a torn piece of a one toman note. The owner glanced at the note, then back at Wick. Then, he reached into his desk drawer, drew out another torn note and laid it down beside the one Wick had produced. The two pieces fit together perfectly. It was an old-school way to determine authenticity in this trade and even in the age of hi-tech gizmos, it still worked like a charm. The shop owner looked at Wick and inclined his head slightly, gesturing for him to go inside.

Wick walked past the man and entered the cramped corridor behind a ragged curtain. A zero-watt bulb dangled before a door at the end of the corridor, dimly illuminating the corridor. Wick paused at the door. It was unlatched. He pushed it open and light spilled out from within. The room was separated into two sections with a long table in the middle. A young man stood on the other side holding a cell phone in his left hand. The shop owner from outside had evidently already informed him about the visitor. As soon as he saw Wick, he pulled a large black canvas bag from the floor and set it down on the table. Wick looked at the boy for a fleeting second and then, without a word, unzipped the bag and made a cursory inspection of its contents. Satisfied, he zipped the bag and lifted it. The weight seemed right too. He drew an envelope from his back pocket and slid it towards the boy. The boy counted the notes within, smiling when he saw the amount was more than that asked. Wick didn't return the smile. He backed out, without breaking eye contact with the boy. Stepping out of the room, he closed the door and crossed the corridor. In less than thirty seconds, he had left the shop and disappeared into the crowd.

# CHAPTER 3

WICK HAD TAKEN utmost care in traveling to the shop, choosing secluded alleyways and inner streets. Still, the whole business deal had taken less than three hours and he was back in the safe house well in time.

Putting the bag down in the dining area, he checked his watch. In a few hours he would be dropped off as close to the target as they could manage. From there he would be on his own.

He had everything laid out and, for the next half hour, he meticulously analyzed the contents of the bag. This routine, which he followed without fail on every mission, ensured no mistakes. It meant that he would not head into war territory only to find his gun jammed, or his ammunition low, or any of the other thousand possibilities that could occur in the heat of combat. He was always coming up with ways to be more efficient on the battlefield. This line of thinking explained the arsenal he chose for his missions. Operatives of his caliber—of which there were few—

often spent hours selecting tailor-made, customized weapons. Not Wick.

He saw nothing but potential problems in guns like that. Most of them were largely untested. He had faced that problem first-hand, ceding control due to a gun malfunctioning during combat and paying dearly for it. He now preferred the toughest, most steadfast arsenal for himself. The weapons that would never in a million years jam on the battlefield.

Over the next thirty minutes, he disassembled all his weapons and checked each part for flaws with extreme patience and care. There was a time for brashness and recklessness, but it wasn't before the mission began.

Olivia entered the safe house when Wick was in the process of re-assembling the guns. Behind her came Logan and Elijah. They nodded at each other and set about their respective tasks with robotic precision.

Ten minutes later, Wick was standing at the right side of the center table with them. Olivia was going over each detail. They had done this already by video conference but doing it in person was critical. The team was very thorough in this regard. They had planned a concise tactical operation order, breaking down the mission to the last detail. Wick's experience of working with the Special Forces teams told him that this team had been with one of the military's elite units.

. . .

"We will be out in forty minutes," Wick stated at the end of the recap.

Then began the standard operating procedure. Before leaving the safe house, all notes had to be burnt. Radio frequencies, escape routes, maps, passwords, codes—everything was committed to memory. Everyone's fake credentials were placed in flash bags. If things went wrong, all they had to do was pull a string on the bag and its contents would be incinerated instantly.

Everything had been planned and rehearsed multiple times, but Wick didn't have a good feeling about this one. He couldn't quite put his finger on the reason for his unease.

He was reminded of a mission, early in his career, where he had been confident about everything and, by the end of it, more than twenty US soldiers were dead. Ever since then, he had never really felt completely confident about any mission. Still, this feeling was different. Was he losing his edge? Maybe. He was just twenty-seven but over the last few years he had been consistently running head-on into dangerous situations and somehow getting out of them alive; and every time something within him changed.

He had been an angry man for so many years and had always used that anger to sharpen his focus, but now the fury was mellowing. He knew that sooner or later this lost intensity would cost him his life. Luckily, he had had no woman in his life so far; flings, but nothing serious. However, that stance was also changing. Now he wanted to feel something different—maybe something on the opposite pole of hatred. Maybe he wanted to put his life as a TF-77 operative behind him and move on. Maybe.

Elijah removed his headphones and announced, "The first set of guests to the convention have arrived."

Wick checked his watch. It was twenty minutes to one, about ninety minutes before the strike. It was time to check with Helms one more time. Wick grabbed the COMSAT mobile phone and carried it to the next room.

▭

**GET WICKED KILL NOW**
**Sam Wick Universe Book #4**

▭

## YOUR FREEBIE

# ACKNOWLEDGMENTS

To my **advance readers group** who are nothing but supportive of my writing and extremely helpful in rectifying mistakes that could have ruined the experience of reading this story.

# ABOUT THE AUTHOR

Dear Fabulous Reader,

Thank you for reading. If you're a fan of Sam Wick, spread the word to friends, family, book clubs, and reader groups online.

*I would love to hear from you. Let's connect @*
*www.thechaseaustin.com*
*chaseaustincreative@gmail.com*

*Join my Facebook group below to get behind the scene content or follow me on Goodreads, Instagram or BookBub.*